bedeviled

CAREFUL WHAT YOU WISH FOR

D0769861

by Shani Petroff
Grosset & Dunlap

An Imprint of Penguin Group (USA) Inc.

GROSSET & DUNLAP
Published by the Penguin Group
Penguin Group (USA) Inc., 375 Hudson Street, New York, New York 10014, USA
Penguin Group (Canada), 90 Eglinton Avenue East, Suite 700, Toronto, Ontario
M4P 2Y3, Canada (a division of Pearson Penguin Canada Inc.)
Penguin Books Ltd., 80 Strand, London WC2R 0RL, England
Penguin Group Ireland, 25 St. Stephen's Green, Dublin 2, Ireland
(a division of Penguin Books Ltd.)
Penguin Group (Australia), 250 Camberwell Road, Camberwell, Victoria 3124,
Australia (a division of Pearson Australia Group Pty. Ltd.)
Penguin Books India Pvt. Ltd., 11 Community Centre,
Panchsheel Park, New Delhi—110 017, India
Penguin Group (NZ), 67 Apollo Drive, Rosedale, North Shore 0632, New Zealand
(a division of Pearson New Zealand Ltd.)
Penguin Books (South Africa) (Pty.) Ltd., 24 Sturdee Avenue, Rosebank,
Johannesburg 2196, South Africa
Penguin Books Ltd., Registered Offices: 80 Strand, London WC2R 0RL, England

Text copyright © 2010 by Shani Petroff. Cover image © 2010 by Penguin Group
(USA) Inc. All rights reserved. Published by Grosset & Dunlap, a division of
Penguin Young Readers Group, 345 Hudson Street, New York, New York 10014.
GROSSET & DUNLAP is a trademark of Penguin Group (USA) Inc.
Printed in the U.S.A.

Cover illustration by J. David McKenney.

Library of Congress Cataloging-in-Publication Data is available.

ISBN 978-0-448-45113-8   10 9 8 7 6 5 4 3 2 1

For Jordan E. Petroff,
a truly remarkable man.
A lot of people say they have the
world's best brother,
but in my case it's true.
I love you.

There are many people who helped make this book a reality.
I'd like to thank:

Judy Goldschmidt, an incredible editor who truly helped Angel and me find
our way. Thank you for your support, time, and top-notch editing skills.

Francesco Sedita, Bonnie Bader, Lana Jacobs, and all the amazing people at
Penguin who worked on Bedeviled. I can't thank you enough.

Cover illustrator J. David McKenney for another great job.

Jodi Reamer, my fabulous agent, for always being in my corner, as well as
Alec Shane and the team at Writers House.

My friends, colleagues, readers, and the librarians and booksellers who've
supported me. It means a lot.

My wonderful family—all the cousins, aunts, and uncles for your
encouragement. My sister-in-law, Andrea, who always knows the right thing
to say. My mom, who is my strongest champion and biggest fan. And my
dad, who always supported my dreams.

You are all in my heart.

chapter

Cole. Daniels. Was. Kissing. Me!

Who needed the devil? My wish was coming true all on its own. That's right. I, Angel Garrett, freak show extraordinaire, snagged the cutest guy in the whole school right out from under Jaydin Salloway's mean but perfect little nose.

And he was kissing me!

Nothing else mattered. Not that I was the daughter of the devil or inherited whacked-out powers that went off at the worst possible moments or even that I was wearing the ugliest dress in the history of dresses at the big school dance.

None of it.

Because Cole chose me. This was totally my Cinderella moment. Well, except for the dress. It really was hideous. I had my powers to thank for that.

But so what? Cole didn't seem to care that I looked like the prom queen from clown school. Which had to be a definite sign he was into me. That, and the fact that HE WAS KISSING ME.

It was like I had little wind gusts twirling around in my stomach that shot to my head and all the way down to my toes. And our lips had only touched for three seconds. But still, they felt all tingly and—

"Mm-hm." The sound of someone clearing their throat interrupted my thoughts—and my kiss.

I expected it to be Jaydin, or worse, her commander-in-chief Courtney Lourde, there to tell me off. To let me know that no one messed with Goode Middle School's in crowd and got away with it and that I should be prepared to pay. *That* I would have been ready for. Courtney and Co. made it their mission to make my life miserable. But this, *this* was way worse. I opened my eyes to see my science teacher, Miss Simmons, hovering over me. Talk about mortifying.

"Break it up," she said.

Not that she needed to. Cole had already jerked his foot away from me as if I had sprayed him with Angel repellant. Miss Simmons just stood there. I could feel my cheeks getting warm, and my eyes darted to the ground. *Can you get detention for kissing?* I honestly had no idea.

"Sorry," I mumbled to her. I didn't want to get Cole in trouble. Not for kissing me. I only wanted him to associate that with good things, like minty-fresh breath and cotton candy lip gloss.

Luckily Miss Simmons didn't lecture us or anything. She just walked away.

I snuck a look at Cole. He had this sheepish smile on his face. "I think everyone may have seen that," he said, stepping back toward me.

He was kind of right. A whole bunch of people were staring at us. And those who weren't seemed to be getting an earful from those who were. It was way embarrassing. Of course, in the grand scheme of things, this was nothing compared to some of the humiliating situations I had gotten myself into in the past. Like accidentally making my shirt disappear in front of everyone—including Cole—and getting the nickname Double-A based on . . . well . . . you can guess why. . . .

"Yeah," I responded. It wasn't the cleverest thing to ever come out of my mouth, but I was at a loss. What if Cole didn't want people to know he liked me? Maybe he just wanted me to be his nerdy little secret that no one knew about.

We stood there looking at each other for a moment.

"Well, I guess that was one way to tell people we're back together," he said, pushing his hair out of his eyes. "We *are* back together, right?"

I didn't even realize I was holding my breath until I let out a huge sigh of relief. Cole wanted me to be his girlfriend again. And he didn't care if the whole school knew. This was the best moment ever! "Definitely!" I told him.

"So no more avoiding each other, right?" he asked.

And just like that, my moment ended. I wanted to say yes. To tell him I wouldn't ignore him anymore. But I wasn't sure I could. The whole reason we stopped hanging out in the first place was that I was afraid to be around him. My powers tended to go off when my emotions went into overdrive, and that happened a lot around Cole. The last time he tried to kiss me, I accidentally set off fireworks in his backyard. But nothing bad had happened this time. Maybe I had everything under control.

I caved. "No more avoiding each other."

Hanging out with Cole was worth the risk.

When he took my hand again, I knew I had made the right call. It was like a shot of warmth surged through me, and I didn't want it to end.

"Good," he said. "I missed hanging out with you."

"Really?" I know he just said it, but I wanted to hear it again.

He nodded, and this time he was the one to look down. Was he getting shy? Around *me*?!

"I missed you, too," I said.

That made him look back up. Our eyes connected, and for a second I thought he was going to kiss me again. But he didn't. Instead, his gaze shifted over to Miss Simmons. Mine did, too. Only I was in for a surprise. Right next to my teacher was my father. Lou was at the dance for everyone to see. The only thing worse than having your father show up to a dance is having your father show up to a dance when your father is the devil.

"Isn't *Zombie Zone Four* opening next Friday?" Cole said, not thinking twice about who was standing next to the punch bowl.

"Yeah." I didn't know what to focus on—what Cole was saying, or that my father, Lucifer himself, was watching everything. What if he had seen Cole kiss me?

"I was thinking we could go," Cole said.

I dropped his hand. I heard regular dads were way overprotective of their daughters. What if a devil dad was worse?

Cole looked from his hand back to me. His smile was gone.

Oh no. He thought I wasn't interested. "I want to go to the movie. With you." I quickly added in the last part. Cole knew I was really into horror movies. He wasn't a huge fan, but he was willing to go because of me. That made the invitation even sweeter.

"You don't have to." He jammed his hands into his pockets.

"I want to." It was time to open up to Cole. To tell him the truth. As much of it as I could, anyway. "I know I'm being weird again," I admitted. "But remember how I told you the dad I hadn't seen for thirteen years reappeared in my life?"

He nodded.

"See that guy by Miss Simmons?"

"The sub?"

"Yeah." Lou had turned himself into our substitute teacher for a day to try and get closer to me. "Well, that's my father."

"No way!"

"Yep, and I had no idea he'd be here spying on me tonight." As if on cue, Lou waved at us, then pointed at his watch.

"Oooh, that stinks," Cole said. "My mom wanted

10

to chaperone tonight, too. I had to beg my father to talk her out of it."

I would have preferred his mom to my dad.

"Looks like he's ready to take you home," Cole said, and nudged his chin toward Lou, who was still pointing at his watch.

"I guess I have to go," I said.

Then Cole started walking. Straight for Lou. "Uhh. What are you doing?"

"Taking you over to your dad."

That's what I was afraid of. "Don't worry about it," I assured him. "He's not very friendly. He doesn't like talking to strangers."

But Cole wouldn't listen.

"Hello there," Lou said, grinning at both of us, flashing his dimples. The ones I inherited from him. "Having fun?" Then his face got serious, and he looked straight at Cole. "Not *too* much fun, I ho—"

"Anyway," I said, interrupting what was sure to be a lecture on kissing. "Shouldn't we get going?"

"It was nice to meet you, sir," Cole said, putting out his hand to my father.

I grabbed it instead. I wasn't letting Cole shake hands with the devil.

"But Ange—"

"See you on Monday," I told Cole as I gave him a light push toward the door. The poor guy looked so confused, but I had no choice but to get rid of him before my dad said something damaging in his presence.

I grabbed Lou by the arm and dragged him out of the dance.

"Well, that was rude," Lou said when we were alone.

"What?"

"You wouldn't even let me shake the boy's hand."

I shrugged my shoulder. "Sometimes when people shake hands, it's to seal a deal. How do I know you're not going to turn around and act like Cole had agreed to some kind of pact in exchange for his soul?"

"Angel, I told you. I'm done with that. I'm a good guy."

"A good guy who still runs the underworld."

Lou shook his head. "Only because I haven't found a replacement yet. *Someone* has to make sure the bad souls are kept in check, and that person has to be very trustworthy—do you know how difficult it is to find a trustworthy person who also aspires to be the devil? But I don't do anything evil. You asked me to stop trading innocent souls for granted wishes and I have."

He looked genuinely sad. "Okay," I said. "I'm sorry."

"You have to trust—"

Just then, Lou's hPhone went off. An hPhone is like an iPhone but with underworldly applications. Access to anywhere on Earth with the click of a button, for example. That's how I accidentally ended up under the dinner table at Cole's house one night.

"It's not a good time," Lou said into the phone. "I'm going to have to call you back."

"Wait," pleaded the voice on the other side. Whoever it was shouted so loudly I could hear everything. "It's important. I need to talk to you."

"It's really not a good ti—"

"You've got to help me," the voice continued. "I did it just like you said. I made him a major leaguer, but something went wrong. I don't know what I did, but now he's also starring in *Swan Lake* at the American Ballet Theatre and has a seat in the Senate. He's trying to pass a bill outlawing the name Susan. People are very upset!"

I stumbled back a few steps. No. It had to be a mistake. My ears were playing tricks on me. Lou had just finished telling me he was done trading the souls of the innocent. Even *he* was past lying straight to his daughter's face. Or so I thought. . . .

"Hanging up now," Lou said before clicking off.

"What was *that* about?" I asked, praying it was nothing.

"Just some silly underworld business. Don't concern yourself with it."

But I couldn't let it go. "What *kind* of business?"

He waved me off. "Just helping make someone's dream come true."

But at what price? People from the underworld didn't go around helping others. Not without getting something in return.

"Angel," Lou said.

But I didn't respond. I couldn't. My whole body was numb, and the blood stopped running through my veins. Because my head understood what my heart couldn't. My father was still evil.

chapter

2

"That was just an old business associate joking around." Lou moved toward me. "Really. Nothing bad."

"Liar," I shouted. "Do not come any closer." My whole body was shaking, not so much from fear, but from anger. How could I have been such a fool? He was Lucifer himself. He made a living deceiving people. He wasn't going to change just for me.

"I know what you're thinking," Lou said.

"You don't know anything about me." My hands clenched into fists.

"You're feeling hurt and betrayed," Lou said, his voice low and soothing. But I wasn't going to be lulled into forgiving him. "But I promise you, I kept my word. I have not tried to take a good soul."

Did he think I was the biggest airhead in North America? "I heard you," I spat.

"No, who you heard was Gremory. He was the one trying to take the soul. Not me. I was just helping him out of a jam."

Seriously? Seriously?! Was his moral compass so messed up that he couldn't tell instructing someone to take a soul was just as bad as taking it himself? Or had he just found a loophole to his promise? "It's the same thing."

"Not technically," he said.

I let out a snort. "You want to get technical? Well, technically, you promised you'd be good. You even got mad at me when I doubted you two minutes ago. But last time I checked, teaching some guy to be evil is not good."

"I didn't teach him to be evil. He already was. He's a demon—that's how they are."

That actually caught me off guard. I never really thought about the other dark beings in the world.

"W-well," I stammered, "you didn't have to help him." My nails stabbed into my palms. I needed to feel the pain. To know this was real, not some nightmare.

Lou lowered his head. "I'll make it up to you. You'll see, I can be better."

I wasn't falling for his fake promises again. "Too late, Lucifer. I want nothing to do with you. Ever."

I started to run off. Only I tripped on my dress and fell forward, skinning my elbows.

Tears sprang out of my eyes before I could stop them.

"Here," Lou said, reaching out to touch my wounds. "I can fix it, make you feel better."

"No, you can't." Because while the fall stung, it was nothing compared to how he hurt me. Without another word, I turned my back on him and walked away.

chapter

3

"There you are," my best friend, Gabi Gottlieb, shouted as she ran to catch up with me. I kept walking without even bothering to turn around and acknowledge her. "I've been looking for you everywhere. It's a good thing that dress is so bright. I could probably see you from Mars. Where are you going, anyway?"

She followed, ignoring the fact that I was ignoring her.

"You're not going to believe what you missed. There were about forty cupcakes left over on the dessert table, and Marc Greyson bet Porter Ciley he could eat all of them. He got to nine before Miss Simmons came over and made him stop. You should have seen him, this light blue frosting all over his face. It was actually kind of cute. Cute-disgusting, anyway." She put her monologue on pause to take a few breaths.

"Will you slow down? I can't keep up. I saw you and Cole . . ."—she lowered her voice to a stage whisper—"kissing. So cool! Does this mean you two are back together for good? Normally, I would totally be against stealing someone else's date. But since it's Jaydin you're stealing from"—Gabi made a gagging noise after her name and then continued talking at superwarp speed—"and she did kind of take him from you, I think it's okay. Besides, you and Cole are meant for each other. So, come on, fill me in!"

"Not now, okay?"

"Whoa." Gabi reached out and pulled on my arm to keep me from moving forward. "Not so fast," she said. "What's going on? You just kissed Cole Daniels. Why do you sound like you just found out you need to have all your teeth pulled without any novocaine?"

"Because Lou lied to me. He never gave up his old ways."

She didn't even know how to respond. "Are you sure?"

"Positive. He's still evil." I choked back a sob. "And maybe that means, deep down, I am, too."

"You are not."

"You don't know that. The seeds of it could be lurking inside me waiting to explode. He and I share half of our DNA."

"Don't be ridiculous." Gabi put both her hands on my shoulders. I thought she was going to shake me. "This is probably all a big misunderstanding. Lou's been trying to get on your good side, he wouldn't risk that."

"Well, he did." I filled her in on everything.

"I'm sorry," Gabi said, and gave me a hug. "But everything will be okay. You were fine before Lou came into your life, and you'll be fine now that he's out of it."

I wished I was as sure.

chapter

4

"Angel," my mom called out to me. "Come on downstairs. It's noon. You can't stay in bed all day."

I dragged myself out of bed as quickly as I could. Otherwise my mom might have forced me to do some hocus-pocus wake-up ritual. That's my mom: into anything new age. It's even her job. She has a website called aurasrus.com where she sells crystals, potions, and other corny products.

"I didn't hear you come in last night. How was the dance?" she asked as I plopped myself down in our big Buddha chair.

"Fine."

"Are you okay?" She studied me, probably looking to see how blackened my aura was.

"Yeah, just tired." I know I could have told her the truth. If anyone could understand what I was going through, it was her. After all, Lou had lied to her a zillion times, telling her he had given up the devil business. But somehow, that made it worse. She had warned me about him, and I didn't listen. It was my fault he was back in our lives, and I didn't need to hear an "I told you so." Not today.

"Are you getting sick?"

"NO!" I jumped to my feet. The last thing I needed was my mom force-feeding me some of her "super secret sleeping potion to knock out illness." Which I was pretty sure was TheraFlu—only chunkier. Mom added her own special touch by throwing in some extra goodies. I think I tasted ginger and maybe eucalyptus. It was hard to tell. But whatever it was, it was definitely gross.

"I'm fine. Really." To prove it, I moved to the fridge. I wasn't hungry, but a healthy appetite meant a healthy girl. At least in Mom's eyes. So I grabbed an apple. "I'm going to go take a walk," I told her.

I didn't even get two blocks before Lou stopped me in my tracks. Literally. His face popped right out of the stop sign. The bright red color made him look like he was wearing one of those devil masks they sell on Halloween. Only he didn't need a mask. He was pure evil all on his own.

"Can we please talk?" he asked.

"No." I didn't want to be near him. But I couldn't get away. When I turned left there he was, sitting on the fence; right, he became the garden gnome; when I went forward he was perched on a mailbox. No matter where I went he was one step ahead of me. "Go away," I shrieked.

"Then talk to me. Let me explain."

I stopped running and faced him. "There's nothing to explain. I don't want to be near you. I don't trust you—or what you'll do."

"We can go somewhere public. Will that help?"

"No."

He ignored my protests, and with a wave of his arm we were in Starbucks.

I gestured toward the handful of people in the store. "Aren't you worried they're going to wonder how we just poofed in here?"

"Not really."

"That's right," I said, crossing my arms over my chest. "You can just erase their memories."

"I told you before that's very dangerous."

"You've said a lot of things that aren't true." I didn't wait to hear him defend himself. I headed straight for the exit. "I'm out of here."

"Angel, wait," he called after me. "Hear me out."

I tried to push the door open, but it wouldn't budge. Not even when I pressed all of my weight against it. But the strangest part? No one noticed. Not even one person bothered to look up at the girl fighting with the front door. Something was up. Something Lou-related. "What did you do?"

He shrugged his shoulders. "I may have cloaked us in invisibility. No one in here can see or hear us."

What good was having people around if they couldn't hear me scream for help? "I thought you said we'd be in public."

"You can still see them. I thought it would make you feel more comfortable," he said. "Isn't that something?"

I was sick of Lou's loopholes—his half-truths. "Undo it."

"I promise," he said, holding up his Boy Scout pledge fingers. "Right after you let me explain."

His word didn't mean much. But it wasn't like I had much choice. "Fine," I said, and dropped into the closest chair. "Talk. You have three minutes. Go."

"What would you like to drink?" he asked, wasting six of his seconds.

"Nothing." A coffee wasn't going to make things better. Not even close.

"Okay. Now I want to explain what you heard before," Lou said, his voice all syrupy sweet. "It wasn't anything bad. Really. That guy you heard on the phone, well, his name is Gremory. He heard I was looking for a replacement, and he wants to take over. He tries very hard, and he was looking for an opportunity to prove himself. So he went out and tried to take a soul. All on his own. I had nothing to do with it. But when things backfired, he came to me for help. I am the expert in the field, after all."

"Yeah, the expert at tricking people," I said, shredding a napkin that was sitting on the table.

"No, the expert at granting wishes. It's very cool actually. With the proper focus you can make someone realize their biggest dreams. Whatever they want is theirs for the taking. They just need to focus really hard on it while I do it at the exact same time. No questions, no strings. Just a perfect wish."

"Yeah, in exchange for their soul."

Lou waved his hand, brushing away the awful truth like it didn't matter. "It's not so bad. It just means they work for me for eternity. I could think of worse things."

I bet he could.

"Besides," Lou continued, "they know what they're

25

getting into. Like that guy Gremory was helping."

Helping was not the word I would have chosen.

"He wanted to be a major-league baseball player," Lou went on. "Now presto. He's an all-star. No one even questions the fact that yesterday he was a nobody. It's an opportunity he never would have had without the underworld."

Lou sounded proud of himself. Like taking a soul was the same as taking a dollar from the guy. It was disgusting.

"Well, *I* have a wish," I said, my hands gripping tightly on the table.

"Anything," he said.

"I wish you would stay out of my life forever."

He gave me a small smile. "You know that won't happen. Besides," he said, his smile spreading wider, "I couldn't grant that even if I wanted to. I'm immune to the wishes of others. They don't work on me. I added that ages ago—as a precaution. Couldn't risk someone wishing to destroy me—or worse—wishing to *be* me."

The last thing the world needed was two Lous. "Your three minutes are up," I said.

"So do you see?" he asked, ignoring what I had just said. "I wasn't doing anything wrong. I was fixing a mistake that someone else made. Someone who wants to take over for me. And the sooner I get someone else up to speed with how my job works, the sooner I can get out of the devil business completely. But I can't just walk away from it. Not without leaving someone I trust in control. Otherwise the underworld would have a power struggle on its hands—everyone trying to be the leader. That would cause a lot of chaos. Even up here on Earth."

"That still doesn't excuse you helping to grant a wish and taking a guy's soul." The napkin I was playing with was now in two hundred little pieces.

"Wish granting isn't bad," Lou said. "It's just giving people what they truly want. That's a good thing in my book. Plus"—he held up his finger in the air for added effect—"these souls seek me and my associates out, not the other way around. That should count for something."

It didn't. Lou could try and put his spin on soul taking any way he wanted, but I wasn't buying it. And I was done being all sad and mopey because of it.

Maybe I couldn't stop him from being evil, but I could make sure I didn't follow suit. I knew what to do. I needed to be the best person ever. A real angel. After all, Kindness is my middle name.

chapter

5

All morning at school on Monday I kept an eye out for ways I could help make the world a better place. And for signs of Lou. (I had warned him to stay away from me, but he wasn't exactly a listen-to-what-you-want type of guy.) I wasn't having any luck. . . .

Until I left gym class. I was one of the last ones out. (I don't like to change in front of people.) There were a couple of guys, including Max Richardson, standing in front of the boy's locker room, and no one looked happy. Especially Max. I decided to investigate. I hid behind the trash can and watched.

"Drop something, freak," Rick Drager said as he shoved Max's books right out of his hands and onto the floor. It made me so mad. How dare Rick treat Max like that!

"Hey, careful," Porter Ciley warned him. "You

28

might make the giant angry. You don't want him to step on you." It was kind of nervy for the guy who played Linus in the school's production of *You're a Good Man, Charlie Brown* to go around picking on someone else. Carrying around a blankie onstage for everyone to see didn't exactly up his cool quotient.

Besides, Max really could step on them. Well, not literally. But he definitely could have swatted them down. He towered over them and everyone else in the eighth grade. Max is pretty massive. He's also the nicest, gentlest, most harmless person ever. But add in that he's awkward, speaks in a whisper, and never stands up to anyone, and unfortunately, you have the perfect middle school target, which is something I know way too much about.

I'm not exactly Miss Popularity. Courtney Lourde, the queen bee herself, would choose swimming in honey with a swarm of hornets coming her direction over hanging out with me. And when Courtney felt that way about someone, they had a better chance of winning Mega Millions five times in a row than securing a spot at the popular table at lunch.

"Are you going to step on me?" Rick said to Max while pushing him until he was smashed up against a locker.

Max didn't say a word. He just stared at his shoes. "Well?"

Do something, Max, I thought. *Defend yourself.* But he just stood there like a snowman. The one the kid down the street was just waiting to decapitate. I couldn't let Max's snowball head roll away. Then it hit me. I could *help* Max. He'd be my first good deed. With a flick of my fingers I sent Rick sailing backward into the lockers on the opposite wall. That would teach him not to pick on people. At least I thought so until I saw Rick's face. His nostrils were flared and his eyes were set directly on Max.

"Did you just push me?" he asked, getting up in Max's face. "Did you?"

I didn't know what to do. Was I supposed to send Rick flying back again? From the looks of things, that would only make him angrier with Max. Did that mean I was supposed to just do nothing? Neither option seemed right.

"I'm talking to you," Rick yelled, slamming Max's shoulders into the locker. "Did you just push me?"

Oh my God. Even my good deeds backfired. I managed to make the situation worse for Max. Maybe I *was* evil.

"Answer me," Rick demanded.

Max shook his head no.

"You look up while I'm talking to you." Rick smacked Max's chin.

I jumped up from behind the trash can. "Leave him alone." It just came out of me. I couldn't help it.

Both Rick and Max turned in my direction, noticing me for the first time. "Aww, look, Max," Rick said. "Do you need a *girl* to come save you?" Porter laughed like Rick had actually said something witty.

"Now before that little freak show goes and tattles on us, tell me you're sorry," Rick instructed Max.

"I'm sorry," Max whispered.

"Louder," Rick said.

"Sorry," Max repeated. I didn't want to watch this; it made me feel as nasty on the inside as Rick was on the outside.

"Good," Rick said. "And if you ever push me again"—he slammed Max into the locker—"you're going to be sorry." Then he walked off with Porter behind him.

And I thought girls were bad.

"Are you okay?" I asked Max as soon as the guys left.

He turned away from me. "I'm fine."

"Are you sure?"

"I'm fine, Angel," he whispered again. But I was pretty sure he was holding back a sob.

I didn't know whether to stay or go. I was afraid my being there was making it worse. Max had been crushing on me since forever. And there was nothing more embarrassing than being humiliated in front of your crush. Another thing I knew all too well . . .

Disappearing shirt. Need I say more?

I didn't want to torture Max the same way. But I couldn't really leave. So we just stood there in silence.

"Do you want to come sit with Gabi and me at lunch?" I finally asked. Max always wanted to do stuff together.

But he didn't take me up on it. He shook his head *no* ever so slightly. "I have to get to my tutoring session."

Then he left, not even making eye contact.

So much for doing good.

chapter

6

"You should have seen it," I told Gabi as I stabbed my spork into my mashed potatoes. "They were absolutely awful. And Max just stood there. There has to be some way to help him."

"Maybe we can spread a rumor that he's Lance Gold's cousin or something," Gabi suggested. Lance Gold was the hottest actor ever.

"No one will buy that. Max is like the opposite of Lance."

She took a long sip out of her juice box. "Maybe we can give Max a total makeover?" Gabi suggested. "Like one of those eighties movies where they help the really geeky kid get a new look, a new attitude, a new everything, and the kid ends up ruling the school."

"You want *us* to do that?" I asked. "Everyone

either ignores us or hates us. What do *we* know about being popular?"

"*You* made it to the A-list."

I rolled my eyes. When my dad first came back into my life, he "helped" to get Courtney and Co. to like me. "For a millisecond. And that was because Lou used his powers."

Gabi paused and then gave me a huge stare-down. "Correct me if I'm wrong, but Lou's not the *only* one with special powers. . . ."

"Yeah," I said. "And when I tried to use them to help Max, I almost got him beat up. Not exactly what I was going for."

"You only tried one thing. Maybe you just need a different approach. A different power," Gabi said, fiddling with the wrapper from her straw.

Was she hinting I try something advanced? I grabbed the wrapper from her. "You know I don't know how to do anything *really cool*. Not properly, anyway. You've seen the problems I've caused."

"Nothing *really* bad ever happened."

Okay, she was obviously having a small case of amnesia. Either that or I accidentally erased her memory. Again. *Not that bad?* I've turned everyone into statues, sent us to outer space, practically destroyed the school musical, and that's not even the half of it."

Gabi started to giggle. I swear, sometimes she had a messed-up sense of humor. "It all worked out in the end," she said. "And come on, some of it was pretty funny."

"Yeah, hardy-har. What's gotten into you, anyway? Since when do you support me trying new powers?"

She twirled her finger around a strand of hair and wouldn't look me in the eye. "Since you don't have Lou to train you anymore." The hair was turning her finger purple. "Without him you kind of have no choice but to learn by trial and error."

"Unless I don't use my powers at all."

That made her look up. "You? Yeah, right. You have no self-control. I give you a day before something *forces*"—she put that world in air quotes—"you to spring into action."

Maybe she had a teeny tiny point. "Fine. Maybe you're right. But it's not like you'd be any different. Probably worse. I bet if you had powers you'd be wishing for a pet unicorn or something."

"Would not," Gabi said, tossing a soy chip at me. "I have self-restraint. If I had your power—"

"Your *what*?"

35

It was Cole. Had he heard what Gabi said?

"Nothing," I assured him, and stuffed some potatoes in my mouth. I needed time to think of something to tell him. And there was no talking with your mouth full.

He took a seat next to me. "Did she say your *power*?"

I practically choked down my food. "No, don't be silly," I said, and gave Gabi a help-me-out-of-here glare. But all she did was give me back an I'm-glad-I'm-not-in-your-shoes stare and bit her lip.

"M-my power," I practically stuttered. "In my house. It went out this morning. I almost missed school because my alarm didn't go off."

"I wouldn't have minded missing first period," he said. "Nothing like a pop quiz to ruin the day."

He bought it. Thank goodness.

"That quiz *was* brutal," I said, not taking my eyes off him. Cole was at my table! He ventured out from popular paradise to the land of Loserville just to be near me. No one ever did that. But Cole was one of the rare few who wouldn't even lose his friends in the process. That's how much everyone liked him.

"Between school and Bar Mitzvah lessons, it's like all anyone expects me to do is study. Can you believe how long our Torah portions are?" Cole said, turning his attention to Gabi. They were in the same class at Hebrew School.

"I know, it's massive," Gabi said as she put her trash into her lunch bag. "I don't know how I'll ever get it down. Or remember the tunes."

I didn't really know what they were talking about, so I just smiled and nodded.

"I can help you with that part. Music is the one thing I do know," Cole said.

"Thanks." Gabi pushed her hair behind her ear. "I'll probably take you up on it."

I know I should have been happy that my boyfriend was making an effort to be nice to my best friend, but I actually felt a little jealous. *I* wanted to be the one he helped.

But there wasn't time to worry about that because my table just kept getting busier. Courtney Lourde and one of her lackeys, Lana Perkins, stopped by. "Cole," Courtney said, putting a phony smile on her face. "Aren't you going to sit with us today?"

"No," Cole said, motioning toward Gabi and me. "There's not enough room for all of us." Did I mention how awesome he was?!

"We can squeeze. I'll make sure everybody feels right at home," Courtney said.

"That's okay," I said.

"Then I guess you'll have to catch the show from over here." She smirked at me and sauntered back to her table.

I didn't have to wait long to find out what she meant. Courtney began doing one of her infamous impersonations. "Please don't hit me, I'm a nice giant," she said in her best Max voice. "I've only eaten three students, and they weren't even the cool ones."

"Leave him alone," she said, switching voices to one that I hate to admit, sounded remarkably like mine.

"Thank you, Double-A, defender of giants and flat-chested girls everywhere," Courtney said, back in her Max voice.

It made me sooo angry. Not just because it stung every time I heard that nickname, but because she was so awful. And no one did anything to stop it.

At least Max had tutoring during lunch and didn't have to see what was going on. But still . . . I was sick of how mean everyone was. Wasn't there enough evil in the world?

chapter

7

"*Je parle, tu parle, ils parl*—I'm never going to get this French conjugation. I should have taken Spanish," I said as Gabi and I were walking to class after lunch.

"You'd have the same problem there. You don't study enough," she said.

"Thanks, Mom." However true it was, I didn't need a lecture. Not from her. Besides, she did enough studying for the both of us. Gabi's mom was majorly into grades. If Gabi didn't come home with As, she had to give up things like TV. Which was a punishment for me, too. My mother hates television, and I'm barely ever allowed to watch it. I depend on Gabi when it comes to my viewing pleasure.

"I'm just saying that if you stud—" Gabi's channeling of Mrs. Gottlieb was cut short as Courtney powered by with Jaydin and Lana in tow. Courtney flipped her hair over her shoulder as she passed, hitting Gabi right in the eye with it. "Uck. How annoying. I don't know why people like her."

"They don't. They're afraid of her." I watched as Courtney forged her way into class. Right as she turned, Max stuck his head out the door. And, like always, he wasn't watching where he was going. Instead of looking ahead, his eyes were on the floor. The two collided—head-on. It was a major train wreck. The kind where you knew there'd be casualties. In this case, it was Max.

Courtney gave him a long, cold stare. Her eyes were slits. "What's your problem?"

"Sorry. It was an accident," Max mumbled. He had one arm on the doorframe. It was like he needed it to steady himself.

"Well, you should be sorry," Courtney said, elbowing him in the gut as she moved past him.

The look in Max's eyes . . . I couldn't take it. It was like Courtney had pulled all the lights out—straight through his pupils. So for the second time in one day, I jumped to Max's defense.

"Courtney," I shouted.

She turned to face me, her hands on her hips. "What do you want?"

Be strong, you can do this, I told myself. It wasn't the first time I went head-to-head with Courtney, but it was never fun. She could be vicious. But someone had to stick up for all the people she hurt. And that someone was going to be me. "Apologize for elbowing him."

"No," she said, keeping her hands on her hips.

"Do it." I took a step toward her.

She took a step toward me. "Who's going to make me?"

Do not show fear, do not show fear. "I am."

My heart was on turbo speed. Did I just challenge Courtney Lourde to a fight? I didn't know how to fight. And I didn't want to. I bruise super easily. But I couldn't back down. People were watching, and I needed to be a hero—for myself as much as for them. I braced myself for the worst. For an elbow to the stomach, a punch to the mouth, a kick to the shin. But it didn't come. Instead, Courtney burst into laughter.

She turned to Lana and Jaydin. "Oh. My. God. How hysterical is that? Double-A thinks she can take *me*." Courtney shook her head. "You know, I thought today was going to be a bust. An English test, boatloads of homework, having to go to school with people like that"—she pointed in my direction—"and

D.L. isn't even here." D.L. Helper was her boyfriend and almost as big a jerk as she was. "But Angel has totally made my day. Watching Double-A defend her true love? Priceless." She walked into class, laughing and mimicking me the whole way. Not once acknowledging me to my face—like I wasn't worthy of being taken seriously.

I was glad Cole didn't take French. I wouldn't have wanted him to hear Courtney squashing me down. Max, on the other hand, witnessed everything.

"Don't listen to a word she says," I told him.

"Yeah," Gabi chimed in. "She's awful. She's said all the same things about me. You just have to ignore her."

Max didn't say anything. He just turned away and went into class, looking defeated.

Just great. I totally embarrassed him. Again. Why hadn't I learned my lesson? He didn't want me jumping to his defense in front of everybody.

A light tapping coming from the debate team's award case made me turn around. Propped up right on the biggest trophy was a miniature Lou, throwing tiny lightning bolts at the glass.

"Not again." When Lou first came into my life, he popped up in school whenever he felt like it.

He promised me he wouldn't do that anymore. But promises, apparently, didn't mean anything to the devil. "I'll meet you in class," I told Gabi.

There were still a few people in the hallway as I made my way to the display case. I tried to use my body to shield Lou and his lightning from any passersby. "You said you'd stay away," I whispered, trying really hard not to move my lips. Explaining to people why I was chatting it up with the trophies was not on my to-do list.

"That was when you agreed to be a part of my life. Agree again, and I'll go."

Lou didn't even try to keep his voice down.

"Shh, I don't need people hearing you." I did a quick glance around. No one seemed to be paying any attention to me. Most were just hurrying to get to class before the late bell or finishing up their own conversations.

"We can always talk later. Just agree to meet with me," Lou insisted.

"No. How many times do I have to tell you?"

"Angel?" It was Reid Winters, Cole's best friend. "Who are you talking to?"

Just what I was trying to avoid. I smashed my whole body against the glass and turned my head to

Reid. "Uh, me?" I stalled. "Nobody. I was just, um, see, it's this thing I do." I was sure Lou was getting a kick out of watching me squirm. "Before French class, I like to look at the debate trophies and give myself a pep talk. It helps give me confidence."

"Cool," he said. But he didn't mean it. The look on his face read "Freak."

I waited for him to leave, but he wouldn't go. He probably wanted to see the full extent of my craziness, so he could run and tell Cole everything. "I just need a few minutes," I said. "I'll be right in."

He shrugged his shoulder and left. I peeled myself off the glass and stared at Lou. "Thanks a lot."

"Don't you mean *merci beaucoup*?"

So not funny. "This is not the way to get on my good side. Get out of here."

Lou winked at me. "I'll win you over, you'll see." He was wrong. But at least he left. Temporarily, anyway. I knew he'd be back. Showing up in school, making my life miserable just for the fun of it. Kind of like what Rick did to Max. Only worse. Lou had powers. He'd make it his new job to bug me. He'd probably even try to get a few of my classmates' souls in the process. Grant them a wi—

That was it! How did I not think of it before? I knew how to help Max.

Wishes.

I had the same capabilities as Lou. Okay, maybe not the same, but close—better even. *I* actually cared about people. And if Lou could grant wishes, I could, too.

Max didn't have to worry about getting bullied anymore. I was going to make his dream come true. He was going to be popular. No soul payment necessary.

chapter

8

It was the perfect plan. Not only was Max going to be on top of the world, I was going to be doing a major good deed in the process.

"Why are you so happy?" Gabi asked as I took my seat next to her.

I was bursting to tell her, but didn't get the chance until twenty minutes later when Mr. Novan let us break into groups to practice speaking French.

"You'll be able to make Max's wishes come true?" Gabi asked.

I looked around the class to make sure no one was listening to us. "I should be able to. When Lou was bragging about his wish-granting abilities, he said all it took was concentration. He and 'his subject' just needed to think about the wish, and it came true. Doesn't sound hard."

Gabi shook her head. "I don't know. Do you really think you can do it?"

I grinded on two of my nails. "I have to try. Why aren't you more excited about this? Weren't you the one who suggested using my powers to help Max?"

"Yeah, but I still don't get how it's going to work."

What was so hard to understand? "I told you," I said, talking super slow this time, hoping it would seep into her brain. "Max just needs to focus on being popular, and I just have to focus on making the wish come true. Simple."

Gabi's lips pursed together.

"What?" I asked.

"How are you going to get him to concentrate on being popular without telling him why? Are you going to fill him in on your family secret?"

She had a point. A really good one.

"Well, no. But I think I know what I can do."

"That doesn't sound like French to me," Mr. Novan said. I hadn't even noticed him creeping up to my desk.

Why did I always get busted? "Sorry."

"*En Français*," he said.

Where was Google Translate when you needed it? "Umm, *désolé*?"

Gabi came to the rescue. She said some stuff that sounded like gibberish until Mr. Novan moved on to torture some other students. It was one of those rare times when I appreciated her mom for being such a homework tyrant—Gabi certainly knew her stuff.

"So, what's your plan?" she asked.

"I can talk to Max about how cool being popular would be. Kind of trick him into thinking about it."

"Way too risky," Gabi said. "You won't know what he's thinking for sure. What if when you bring up the idea of popularity, he starts wishing he were the main character in a popular video game? Then there'd be space monsters with lasers running around the school making people's intestines pop out."

Gabi was right. My plan was flawed. I had to figure out something better.

All through class, I couldn't stop watching Max. It was a good thing Cole didn't have French with me. He would have thought I was crushing on Max. But I couldn't turn away. Mr. Novan had shoved him in a group with Dana Ellers and Tracy Fine. None of them looked happy about it. The girls were squished on one side of the desk, trying hard not to make eye contact with him or even acknowledge he was there. And Max, well, he looked like a golden retriever that someone just swatted with a newspaper. But even sadder. So much so that I wanted to give him a hug. And I've never wanted to give Max a hug.

When the bell rang he got up and shuffled out of class. His head was drooped so low he looked a foot shorter than usual.

"Come with me," Gabi said, her voice sounding chipper. I don't know how. Watching Max made me want to listen to depressing music and cry.

I followed Gabi into the bathroom. She looked under each of the stalls to make sure no one was there.

"What's going on?" I asked. "We have to get to English. I want a seat next to Cole." There were no assigned seats in class. It was first come, first serve.

"Yeah, I know. You have a boyfriend now. Lucky."

"You will, too."

"Yeah, right." Her voice sounded sad, but it quickly perked right up. "But that doesn't matter now." She paused for effect. "You're going to love this. You looked all mopey and down in the dumps over your Max problem. So"—she clapped her hands together and squealed—"I, your incredibly smart best friend, came up with a solution. I know how we can help Max."

Gabi was on her tippy toes, she was so excited. "How?"

"I can wish for everyone in school to like him."

"And how's that going to help anything?"

Gabi pretended to slam her head on the bathroom counter. She had a slight tendency for the overdramatic. "How can you not see?" she asked, straightening back up. "It's your plan, only substituting me instead of Max. *I* can wish that he becomes popular and you can make it come true. That way we know nothing crazy will happen because we'll both be focused on putting him on the A-list."

No wonder I liked Gabi. The girl was a genius.

"Let's do it!" I had her stand directly across from me. We grabbed hands and made eye contact. "Focus," I told her. She nodded.

"Make everyone in school adore Max," Gabi said. "Make the wish come true." I repeated exactly what she said, then concentrated on making her wish come true. *Make Gabi's wish come true. Make Max popular. Make the wish come true,* I thought over and over again. When the late bell rang we dropped hands. "Keep your fingers crossed," I said. "If that worked, we just turned Max's world around."

chapter

9

I didn't have to worry about getting a seat when I got to English class. They were pretty much all empty. Except for the back right hand corner. Right where Max sat.

People were fighting to get a seat near him. My wish granting had worked! I grabbed Gabi's arm. "How cool is this?"

"Totally," she said.

Jaydin squeezed her way into the seat next to Max.

"Get up," Courtney said, yanking her BFF's sleeve. "I want to sit there."

"Too bad," Jaydin said, doing the unthinkable and defying the ever-powerful Courtney Lourde herself. "I got here first."

"I said get up!"

That was something I never expected to see. Not if I lived to be 125 years old. Courtney Lourde fighting to get closer to Max Richardson. I half expected to see Wilbur the pig fly by the window.

"Why don't I make it easy?" Rick Drager said. "Both of you leave him alone. Hey, Max, come check this out. I got a bunch of new rookie baseball cards. Some I already have. You can have the duplicates if you want." Rick? The very Rick who just this morning smashed Max into a locker was now vying for his attention?

When Max didn't move, Rick got up and went to him.

"No way," Cole said, blocking his way. "Everyone knows what you did to him. You think I'd let you get anywhere near him after that?" Cole turned his attention to his new friend. "Don't worry. He tries to mess with you, he has to mess with me first."

"And me," Reid said. A bunch of others echoed him.

This was better than I expected. The whole class was pro-Max. More than that. They thought he was the greatest thing ever. I was so happy I wanted to do a victory lap. After all, my powers let me help someone. Someone who really deserved it. That was definitely high-five worthy.

"All right, everyone, take your seats," Mrs. Torin said.

No one budged.

"The bell rang," she said. "To your desks, or tomorrow there will be a seating chart."

"Oooh," Lana said. "Can you make sure to put me next to Max?"

"That's not fair," Tracy said. "I want to be next to him."

"Okay, okay," Mrs. Torin said as the rest of the class also put in their requests. "I understand. It's not every year I get a student like Max. He is one of a kind."

"Even Mrs. Torin is on a Max kick," Gabi whispered to me as we took our seats—on the empty side of the room. Fortunately, we weren't under the Max spell. I guess that's how it works—the wisher (if the wish isn't on their own behalf) and the granter have immunity. "This is unbelievable."

It really was.

"Max, you can come right up here," Mrs. Torin said. "Take my seat, so everyone can see you."

Max didn't move.

"Come on." Mrs. Torin gestured toward him. "Prize students deserve the spotlight."

Max shuffled his way to the front. He kept his face

down, so I couldn't see his expression. But he had to be hiding a huge smile. Sudden turns in status like this didn't happen all the time.

With Max out of the seating equation, everyone grabbed a desk. Cole took one next to me, which was cool.

"We're going to read aloud from *Romeo and Juliet* today. Max, you can be Romeo. Do I have a volunteer for the part of Juliet?" Mrs. Torin asked.

Every girl's hand shot up except for Gabi's and mine.

"Please," Courtney said, practically lunging from her seat.

And Mrs. Torin actually picked her. Not that I was shocked. She thought Courtney was an amazing actress. She even gave her the lead in *Charlie Brown* not too long ago. The part that should have gone to Gabi.

Watching Max read his lines was pretty torturous. Brad Pitt he was not. He fumbled over the words and took about three million centuries to get out a line. I already thought reading Shakespeare was boring, but listening to it with Max as the lead was way, way worse. Not that anyone else seemed to think so. They applauded every time he managed to spit out a line, and Mrs. Torin even suggested he try out for the next school play!

My special gift was obviously pretty powerful. Maybe I'd try to broker world peace next. The thought made me laugh. Some girls tried to make their fathers proud of them. My goal was the opposite. Lou was going to be furious when he saw all the good I did.

Gabi tossed a note at me.

I carefully opened it under my desk. *This is awesome*, it said. *We did it.*

As I wrote my response, Mrs. Torin called me out. "Something you'd like to share with the class, Angel?"

I crumpled up the paper and dropped it into my backpack. "No, thanks," I said. "They already know."

And they did. I was going to write, *Max is the king!*

chapter

10

"You're in a good mood," Mom commented when I got home.

Understatement. I was in a fantastic mood. I had done something amazing with my powers. Something kind. Or, more importantly, something not *evil*. Nothing was going to get me down. I even volunteered to help Mom with her monthly cleansing. The one where she lights candles and roams through the house shaking a giant totem pole to ward off negative spirits.

The giant pole and I pirouetted around the kitchen. I tossed it up in the air, caught it, and did a dip for an encore. It was *Dancing with the Stars*-worthy. Well, if I was a star.

"What's gotten into you?" Mom asked.

"Just had a good day at school."

"Well, I'm certainly not complaining," Mom said.

"Feel free to waltz your way through the upstairs. It could use a nice cleansing."

I twirled my way into the living room. The totem pole wasn't as much fun to dance with as Cole, but I could pretend. I glided my way upstairs with my partner and did a flying leap into my room.

And then my mood took a sudden nosedive. Try and guess who was leaning against my dresser waiting for me.

I shut the door so Mom wouldn't hear, then I pointed the stick at Lou. "Leave."

"Angel—"

"No, I don't want to hear it."

"What about your lessons?" he asked.

"Don't need them. Don't need you." And it was true. My powers hadn't gone off on their own at all since he was out of my life. Not to mention that I just had major success with wish granting. I was doing just fine.

"What happens when something goes wrong?"

I shook the totem pole at him. "It won't. And if it does, I'll fix it. Maybe I'll just grant myself a wish for everything to be fine. Isn't that what you like to do? Play with wishes?"

"Angel." Lou's face got serious. "Wish granting is

not meant for someone at your level. You need to keep studying with me before you attempt that."

I rolled my eyes at him. He was such a liar. Wish granting was simple. He just wanted me to ask him for help. "Whatever."

"I mean it, Angel. It's very risky to use powers that are beyond your grasp. Do I need to remind you of the time you turned your friends into statues?"

"No."

"And it's not just you," he said. "Take Gremory. He tried wish granting, and he lost control. Then he couldn't undo the damage."

"Well, I'm not a demon."

"No, but you're a girl who doesn't know how to control her powers."

I squeezed the totem pole. It took all my willpower not to tell Lou he was wrong, that I'd already granted a wish, and it all worked out perfectly. But I didn't want him to go and undo it. Or worse, try to make Gabi hand over her soul as payment.

"Promise me you won't try it," he said.

"Fine. I promise." Lou wasn't the only one who could lie.

"Good. Because there can be major consequences. When Gremory tried to undo the wish and the problems he caused—he made a bigger mess."

I knew what Lou was doing. Giving me a lecture to scare me from trying anything advanced without him.

"Yeah, whatever," I said. "Undoing powers is tricky." It wasn't like I had plans to undo anything, anyway. Max was going to stay popular forever. "Got it. Now go."

I pounded the totem pole on the ground.

"Angel."

I pounded again. "Go!"

With that, Lou shook his head and left.

"Are you okay up there?" Mom called out.

"Yep," I answered. "Just getting rid of all the evil in the room."

chapter

{ 11 }

"Can you believe he tried to get me all paranoid about my powers?" I complained to Gabi as we walked into homeroom. "What a jerk."

"Definitely." But she was barely listening to me anymore. Couldn't really blame her, though. I had been talking about it an awful lot. Nonstop, actually. "Hey, look," she said as we got closer to her desk. There was a cupcake with blue icing there. And a folded note.

"What's that?" I asked.

"A cupcake," Gabi said, picking it up.

"I know that. I mean the note. What does it say?"

She shrugged her shoulder and unfolded the piece of paper. "Something sweet for someone sweet," she recited. "From your secret admirer."

Talk about corny. But I didn't say that out loud. Gabi looked superexcited, and I didn't want to ruin it for her. Because corny or not, it was still pretty cool. "Who do you think it's from?" I asked.

"No idea." She put her finger in the frosting and licked it off. "Mmm. I love frosting."

Gabi loves *anything* sweet. But her mom is like the food police and only wants Gabi to eat things with nutritional value. So getting junk food totally made her day. And this particular junk food was from a boy, so it made it that much yummier.

I scanned the room. "Maybe Marc Greyson gave it to you," I whispered. "Wasn't he the one who ate about a dozen cupcakes at the dance? Maybe they're like his signature now. And he seems to be looking this way."

Gabi didn't say anything. She was focused on the cupcake.

"I bet he likes you and wants to go out with you." I had to admit, I was getting pretty excited myself. The thought of Gabi and I going on double dates was totally cool. Maybe one day we'd even have a double wedding.

Gabi turned around to look at Marc. "He is cute. But why would he like me?" She sat down.

I smacked her arm. "Because you are amazing. Why wouldn't he like you? You're smart, you're pretty, you're talented, you're—"

"A big loser," she said.

"Stop it," I hissed at her. "First, you are *so* not a loser. Since when do you believe what Courtney Lourde says? And second, Cole goes out with me. And if you're a loser, then I am, too. And he doesn't seem to care. So then Marc wouldn't, either."

Gabi giggled. "Okay, maybe you're right." She turned around to look at Marc again. "Do you think it could be him? He's *really* cute!"

"Who?" Tracy butted in. "Are you talking about Max? You're friends with him, right?"

I shrugged my shoulder. We weren't exactly friends, but he did follow me around a lot. "I guess."

"Then will you see if he likes me?"

Tracy was asking me for a favor? I thought she hated me! I told her I would. Bringing a couple together was a good thing. And good was my new specialty.

Everything was going just great. Max was even going to get a girlfriend. I didn't know what Lou was talking about. Wish granting was easy. Not sure what Gremory's problem was all about. What do you expect from a demon?

But I certainly was no demon.

I was 100 percent good. And there'd be no mess-ups on my watch.

chapter 12

"Sign this." Courtney shoved a paper under my nose at the end of social studies class.

"What is it?"

She let out a sigh. She clearly didn't want to be talking to me. The feeling was mutual. "A petition. To hold a reelection for student senate."

"Why?" I asked, pushing away the paper she had shoved in my face.

"Duh. So Max can run for president. He shouldn't have to wait until next year. He deserves it now. I already have eighty signatures."

"I'll sign," Rick said, grabbing the paper. He dropped it back in front of me when he was done.

"Now you," Courtney demanded.

I didn't argue. I just signed. So did Gabi. Then Courtney ran over to Max. "Once I have one hundred

63

signatures, I'm going to show it to the principal. I know he'll let us do a revote. You're going to be the perfect president," she said, and flipped her hair over her shoulder, giving Max a big old smile.

Gabi's body was shaking from trying to hold back her laughter. It *was* pretty funny watching Courtney flirt with the guy she once referred to as uglier than toe fungus.

"Courtney," D.L. yelled from the doorway. "What are you doing with *that*? Let's go."

She stood up and marched right over to D.L. "*That* is Max and don't ever speak about him in that tone again. Because I promise, if you do, we are so done."

"What's with you?" he asked, reaching for her hand. "Since when are you champion of the charity cases?"

Okay, this was weird. Why wasn't D.L. on the Max bandwagon?

I wasn't the only one wondering . . .

"What did I just tell you?" Courtney yanked her hand away from him. "Quit being so mean. Why can't you be more like Max?" She stomped out of the room with D.L. following close behind.

"Whoa," Gabi said.

I had to second that. Courtney just dissed the hot school bad boy—her very own boyfriend—to stand up for the freaky school dork. I really did use my powers for good.

Max stood up and walked right past us.

"Wait up," I called out to him.

He stopped, but he wouldn't look at me. Just at his feet.

Okay. I wasn't looking for a "thank you" or anything like that. After all, Max had no idea that I was responsible for his fabulous new reputation. But I would have liked to have seen a smile. A little bounce in his step. Something to prove using my devil powers was worth it. That it had meaning. But nope. Max looked gloomier than ever.

"What's wrong?" Gabi asked.

"Everything," he muttered.

"Everything?" I repeated after him. "What do you mean everything? Everyone is crazy about you. It's like the perfect day."

"Yeah," he said, kicking his foot over a scuff mark in the floor. "Just perfect. Now the whole school is out to get me."

"What are you talking about?" I asked. This was crazy. Was he living in some parallel universe? Our classmates were treating him like a superhero. Gabi's wish made sure of that.

"You've seen it. They're all pretending to like me. It's a big set-up. They're planning something. I'll probably wind up taped to my locker at the end of the day if I'm lucky. It's probably much worse than that. Like this whole president thing. It's some elaborate scheme."

"No," I said. "Max, they just like you."

"Right." His foot moved like crazy over the floor. "All of a sudden, just like that," he said, snapping his fingers, "they start liking me. No way."

I chewed on my nails. This was not what I imagined.

"It could happen," Gabi said, nodding wildly.

Max gave her a weak smile. "No it couldn't. What's worse, even people like Cole and Reid are in on it. It wasn't like we were friends, but at least they never tried to torture me before. Now they're helping Courtney and everyone set me up."

"Cole wouldn't do that," I protested.

"Then why all of a sudden did he offer to help me get ready for basketball tryouts? He barely ever speaks to me. Now he wants to be my friend? He's probably in charge of luring me somewhere."

"It's not like that, Max. It's—" I cut myself off.

"It's what?"

66

What could I say? "It's because of me and my devil powers"? That "I made everyone want to be friends with you"? So I just told him that I didn't know.

Max didn't say anything else. He just walked out of class.

"This is awful," I said to Gabi. My nails were now nonexistent.

"It's not that bad," she said. "Eventually he'll realize everyone's sincere, and he'll be happy."

Eventually? I didn't want eventually. "But *now* he feels worse about himself. And I caused that."

"It'll all work out," Gabi said. "Now come on, let's go. Maybe we'll get to see Marc on the way to class!"

How could she think about boys when Max's future was at stake? "Gabi, this is major. Look how upset he is. He'll probably drop out, beg his mom to homeschool him, and if she says no, he'll just run away from home."

"You're way overreacting," Gabi said.

"I'm not! It could happen. Max needs to know this is real."

"Getting him to believe that right now is going to be hard," she said. "I can't believe I'm actually saying this, but I wish he was more like Courtney. She has enough confidence for the both of them."

"Seriously." My head was pounding. What good was granting Max popularity if he completely misinterpreted it?

chapter

✦ 13 ✦

"I think he smiled at me," Gabi said as we passed Marc on our way to class. "Or maybe it was meant for Brooke. She was right behind me. Did you see it? What do you think? 'Cause if he did smile at me, then he probably was the one to give me the cupcake." Marc was all Gabi could talk about.

I, on the other hand, was more concerned about Max.

"Groups of four," Miss Simmons said. Everyone clamored around Max begging him to be in their group.

"Max," I called out. "Come work with us." I figured it was the least I could do. He knew Gabi and I would never be part of a scheme to set him up. And it would give me time to make him understand that everyone really did like him.

"Riiiight," a voice said back. A voice that sounded like Max's, if Max's voice was sarcastic, evil, and totally condescending. I had to be hearing things.

Only it didn't stop. "No one wants to work with you, Double-A!" the voice that sounded like Max's continued. "Except maybe your nerdy sidekick." Courtney and Co. laughed like they were watching a Will Ferrell movie.

Was this really coming from Max? The Max who has been crushing on me since forever? The Max who tried to carry me home when I fell off my bike in sixth grade? The Max who gave me a homemade present for Christmas every year since I've known him? The Max who was the kindest person in all of Goode? The Max who just moments ago thought the whole school was out to get him? Were the insults really coming from him?

"No way I'd work with you," he said. "Or your spazzy best friend."

Yep. They were. I felt like the Easter bunny just spit on my sneakers.

"Hey," Cole said, stepping up to my defense. "Cut it out."

Max put up his hand. "Look, Cole. We all know you're into doing charity work, and Angel's your pet project, but it doesn't mean the rest of us need to be nice to her. You're lucky we still include you at all."

Cole opened up his mouth to say something else but stopped himself. He just backed into his seat. Then he said sorry. Only it wasn't to me. It was to Max! Apparently nobody talked back to the new Max. Not if they wanted a social life.

"Max?" Gabi said, gripping her braid.

"Gabi?" he said, mimicking her.

"What's going on?"

"Well, at this very moment, it seems I'm having a conversation with the queen nerd's number one subject."

Gabi's mouth fell open and Max laughed. He didn't care that he had just majorly insulted us both. It didn't bother him at all. In fact, it was the opposite. He seemed to stand a whole foot taller.

"Enough," Miss Simmons said. "Groups *now*. Or I pick them. Max, go ahead and choose your partners."

King Max eyed every student, each of whom seemed to be holding their breath.

"Pick me." Courtney broke the silence. "We can go over your election campaign."

"And me," Jaydin added. "I have the best grades in the class."

"No, I do," Kyle Manning countered. "Pick me."

The whole class erupted again trying to point out why they should be chosen. "I made my decision," Max said. Everyone got silent. "Courtney, Jaydin, and Kyle."

There were a bunch of groans. Kyle pounded his fist into the air and yelled "Yes," and Courtney and Jaydin actually squealed. And not tiny ones, either. It was like they just won a Teen Choice Award and an actual Jonas Brother was handing them the surfboard trophy.

"Courtney," D.L. said, running his hand through his hair.

"What?" She looked annoyed that he'd interrupted her before she had a chance to give her big acceptance speech. And Courtney was no Taylor Swift. She'd put anyone in their place.

"Aren't we working together?" D.L. asked.

"We don't need to do everything together. I'm working with Max."

"Then what am I supposed to do?" D.L. asked.

Courtney shrugged her shoulder. But Max gave him an answer. "Join the nerd herd." He gestured toward me and Gabi.

"Yeah, right." D.L. said. Instead, he tried to team

up with a group of guys in the back. But they wouldn't take him.

"Sorry, dude," one of them told him. "What Max says goes. And he wants you to work over there."

D.L. flung his backpack over his shoulder and made his way over to me. He did not look pleased. At all. "Garrett," he said, slamming his bag on the table next to mine. He was so upset about the whole Courtney/Max situation he didn't even bother to insult me.

My group, Gabi, Cole, and D.L., stood there not saying a word.

Can you say awkward?

Gabi finally chimed in, trying to break the tension. "We'll get the microscope." She dragged me from the table. "Okay, what is going on?" she asked me when we were away from everyone.

I shook my head. "Uhh. We created a monster."

"But how? Just last period he was all 'poor me.' Now he's all Freddy Kruger. But meaner."

"Yeah. I don't get it. He even makes Courtney seem nice." Then I had a thought. A bad one.

Popularity hadn't gone to Max's head. Powers had.

"What?" Gabi asked. "You look like you just saw Godzilla."

73

"He's *like Courtney*," I whispered, practically choking on the words.

"No kidding."

I gripped her wrist hard and squeezed. "You don't get it. When we left class you wished he was more like Courtney—and now your wish came true."

chapter

14

"Oh my—" Gabi wrapped her arms around herself. "We turned Max into Courtney!"

I nodded, although it was more me than her. If I didn't have devil blood running through me, none of this would have happened. There'd be no wish granting. No chances for someone nice and kind to be transformed into a monster.

"Okay," Gabi said. "It was just an accident. We must have both been wishing for the same thing at the same time and kicked your wish-granting powers into gear again. It's not a big deal. We'll undo it. Put him back to normal."

But we didn't get a chance. Just then D.L. called us over. "What's taking you so long? Come on."

As much as I hated the idea, Max was going to have to stay Mean Max until lunch.

Science dragged on, and I couldn't stop watching the clock. Counting the seconds until I could undo my mistake.

"Perfect," Miss Simmons said, studying Max's worksheet. "Class, look over here. Now this is the epitome of an amazing student. You should all strive to be more like this young man. Even when his answers are wrong, you can tell thought and effort went into them."

D.L. snorted. Almost everyone gave him a nasty stare. "Okay, what am I missing?" he asked. "Is everyone in a trance or something? Why is everyone all about Max? Even Simmons is gushing."

The bigger question was why wasn't D.L.? Once I took a moment to think it through, I realized he'd been on Courtney that whole time for the way she was treating Max. Gabi and I weren't affected by the wish because we were the ones responsible for it. But D.L.?

"Cole?" I said, my fingers crossed. "Why do you think everyone likes Max?"

"Because he's awesome. I hope he joins the basketball team. It would be so cool to ha—"

I stopped listening as he blathered on about Mr. Wonderful and turned my attention back to D.L. "You really don't think Max is cool?"

"No. I don't get why anyone else does, either. I swear I'm absent one day, and it's like I come back to the Twilight Zone."

"You were absent?"

He didn't need to answer. I knew the answer. I remembered Courtney mentioning it. She was all upset that he wasn't in school the other day.

Then it all started to make sense. Gabi had wished for everyone *in* school to think Max was amazing. But D.L. wasn't here, so the wish didn't affect him.

It was the first piece of good news. At least the whole world wouldn't be bowing down to some eighth-grader from Goode, Pennsylvania. Since I barely spoke to my mother last night, I never had the chance to see if she, or anyone outside school, had been sucked into the vortex of Max worship. This was a relief. Only people who were in the building were stuck that way. At least until I could fix it.

A roar of laughter came from Max's table. "I can't believe I never knew how funny you were before," Courtney told our school's new ruler.

"There's a lot you don't know."

It was clearly a dig, but Courtney just beamed at him.

D.L. put his elbows on the desk and rested his head on one of his hands. "I don't get it. Why would she want to hang out with him over me? I mean, look at him."

It was hard to feel sorry for someone who was even conceited when he was sad. I shrugged a shoulder. "Maybe everyone is finally realizing how great Max is."

But as I watched Max point to Gabi and laugh, I felt like I got punched in the stomach. Max wasn't great. He was awful. And he had the devil's daughter to thank for that.

chapter

15

"That better have worked," I said. Gabi and I were sitting at our table in the cafeteria, and I had just finished trying to reverse her last wish. We both chanted "Make Max nice again" about thirty times. I couldn't take another minute of his meanness. I actually missed the clumsy old version of him shuffling up behind me on my way to class.

"It did," Gabi said, grabbing her lunch. "It had to." She looked at the closed bag in her hands. "Please make it be something good today. I can't take anymore tofu burgers." She held it out to me. "Want to trade?"

"No way." I was going to stick with my grilled cheese sandwich and greasy potato chips.

"Whoa!" Gabi pulled out her food, but it wasn't what she—or I—expected at all. It was junk food deluxe. A cheeseburger, french fries, a Twix bar, and even a can of Coke. "I think my mom might be having a nervous breakdown." She popped a few fries in her mouth. "But I'm okay with that if it means this is what I get for lunch," she said, her mouth full. "These are sooo good."

"I can't believe she gave you that. What happened to fast food stunting your growth, poisoning your body, muddying your mind, and doing whatever other damage she could think of?"

"Maybe my dad packed it. I could totally see him trying to surprise me."

"I should have traded," I said, letting go of my sandwich, which suddenly didn't look as appealing, onto my tray.

"Too late now," she gloated, and took a bite of her cheeseburger.

"Hey," Cole said, sitting down and grabbing a few of Gabi's fries and downing them. He gave her one of his huge lopsided smiles. "You don't mind, right?"

How could she mind? Not after getting one of those smiles. They were pretty irresistible. And she was human, after all.

"Nope," she said, gesturing for him to take more.

"Sweet. Thanks." Cole took more of her lunch. "When do you want me to help you with your Bat Mitzvah stuff?"

"Everyone ready for Mrs. Torin's test today?" I chimed in, totally changing the subject. I was feeling left out. And I wanted him to make plans with me. Not my best friend.

"Ughh," Gabi said. "No. There was so much reading. I—" She didn't finish because she got distracted. We all did.

Max had marched right into the center of the lunchroom and now he was standing *on* Courtney's table. Gabi and I exchanged a look.

It was safe to assume that the reversal didn't work.

"Uh-oh," Gabi whispered. "What's he doing here, anyway? I thought he had math tutoring during lunch."

"And disappoint his minions?" I asked.

"Angel," Cole reprimanded me. "You shouldn't talk about Max like that. He's my friend."

I knew it was the spell talking and not Cole, but it made me want to give him a hard poke, anyway. Max had totally ripped on me in science class. Powers or no powers, Cole should hate him for the sheer fact that I'm his girlfriend and Max dissed me. But no. Cole didn't want to defend *me*. Just his idol.

He even left me stranded at the lunch table. He wanted to go sit near Max. So he just stood up, waved a quick good-bye, and ran back to his old table. Correction. Make that Max's table.

"I decided to join you all today," Max said, perched on the tabletop. Applause sounded throughout the cafeteria. Even the lunch ladies joined in. "I don't feel like standing in line, so I need someone to go pick up my lunch." About a dozen people jumped up. "You," Max said, pointing to Dana. "And it better be decent."

Instead of being annoyed that he was acting like some cruel drill sergeant, she practically skipped off to go get his food. She didn't even care that he didn't give her money for it. I half expected him to ask people to lick his shoes clean. He probably would have if someone gave him the idea. "And since I'm missing my math lesson, I'm going to need someone to finish my assignment for me."

"I can do it," Jaydin said. "I'm great with equations. And I can tutor you if you want."

"I'll think about it," Max said.

Think about it? One of the prettiest, most popular, and smartest girls just offered to help him in a subject he stunk at, and he was going to *think about it*?

"Let's try again," I told Gabi. "We need to reverse this."

We grabbed hands. The good thing about sitting at

the nerd table was that no one paid attention to you. Well, unless they wanted to make fun of you. But everyone was too wrapped up in Max to even notice we existed.

"I wish Max was back to his normal self," Gabi said.

I repeated it, squeezing Gabi's hands so hard she actually yelped. "Please, please, please, let him be normal again," I prayed. Never in my life had I concentrated on anything so hard. This needed to be reversed. I was not going to be responsible for causing more evil in the world.

"Please, let him be nice again." This time I said it about three hundred times. No exaggeration.

"Max, come sit next to me," Courtney said. "Move, D.L." She swatted her boyfriend's arm. "Give him some room."

Max jumped off the table and stood over D.L. "I don't like to be kept waiting."

"I don't believe this," D.L. said, getting up from his seat.

Neither did I.

The reversal didn't work.

chapter 16

"Look," Gabi said, running over to her locker. There was a note taped to it. She definitely was not as concerned about this whole Max situation as I was, which was pretty frustrating.

"Oh my gosh!" she exclaimed. "I bet it's from my secret admirer." She tore it down. "It is," she said, and actually jumped a foot into the air.

GABI, G=GRACIOUS. A=AMAZING. B=BEAUTIFUL. I=I HOPE YOU'LL FEEL THE SAME WAY ABOUT ME.

"How are you supposed to feel the same way if you don't even know who it's from?" I muttered, leaning my back against the locker.

"Don't be such a downer," she said, smacking my knuckles with the note. "This is the most exciting thing that has happened to me in . . . in . . . ever! The only thing that would make this day better would be if we didn't have to take that English test."

"Uh . . . and how about Max? We have to figure out how to fix him."

She clutched her note. "I know. We'll figure it out. Or, and I know you don't want to, but maybe we can just ask Lou for help?"

"How can you even suggest that?" My eyes darted around the hall. Just saying my father's name was enough to make him come pay me a visit, and I was in no mood. "He's not a part of my life anymore. Not after what he did."

Her voice got extra quiet. "But he wasn't the one who set out to take anyone's soul. From what it sounds like, he was just trying to clean up that other guy's mess."

"But he didn't *have* to step in. He could have just walked away from the whole situation." How could she side with the devil? "I can't forgive him. Not this time."

"Okay," Gabi said. "Sorry I said anything. I promise, we'll come up with a different solution."

I nodded. "Maybe we just need to go somewhere really quiet to reverse everything."

"Maybe," she said, "but first, we have to get through English. I need an A on this test, so my mom doesn't kill me. What I wouldn't give for us to get out of class today."

She didn't need to tell me. Gabi was a much better student than I was. "There you are," Mrs. Torin said when Gabi walked into class. "I've been waiting for you."

Gabi's eyes froze with fear. It was like watching a hunter pick up a gun and point it at Bambi's mother. "Is everything okay?" she asked.

"More than okay," Mrs. Torin said. "As a reward for being such an exemplary student, you don't need to take today's test. You have an automatic A. In fact, you can leave early. I'll write you a pass. And that's not all. . . ."

Mrs. Torin looked at me. "This is your lucky day, too, Angel. Gabi should have someone to celebrate with, so you can go home as well."

She was letting us both leave? Normally I would have been ecstatic. But not this time.

This wasn't good news. Not good news at all.

chapter

17

"Oh my God. Oh MY God. OH. MY. GOD."

What had I done?

"That was so awesome," Gabi screamed as we left school, skipping out on last period. But she couldn't have been more wrong. That wasn't awesome, that was completely horrendous.

"I cannot believe she just let us leave," Gabi chirped away, oblivious to the disaster unfolding around us. "What's going on today?"

"You. You're what's going on."

"What are you talking about?" she asked.

"Yes, what are you talking about?" Lou was standing right in front of us! I put my arm out to block Gabi from him. He was dangerous. There was no way I was letting him near my best friend.

"None of your business!" I shouted.

"Isn't it a little early for you to be done with classes?" he pressed on. "Cutting school are we?" He looked amused.

"No!" I couldn't blame him for thinking I was a juvenile delinquent, following in dear old dad's footsteps. "Gabi isn't feeling well," I lied. "So the nurse gave me permission to take her home. What are you doing here, anyway?"

"Well, you said you didn't want me visiting you in school. So I waited for you outside."

"I don't want you visiting me *anywhere*!" I needed him gone. And not just because I hated being around him. But because I needed to warn Gabi about what I did. To her! Without Lou finding out.

"Now, now," he said. "Don't be so quick. I can be useful. I can help your friend get better. Gabi, what would you like? Chicken soup? Or I can whip you up some cold medicine that tastes like chocolate-dipped strawberries. Or maybe you just need some relaxation. How about a spa day?"

"Gabi, don't even think about accepting any of that," I warned.

"Fine," she said to me. "But some of it does sound good. I wish—"

I covered her mouth with my hand. "Think about

Max. How he acted in science class. Seriously. Just think about Max."

Lou raised an eyebrow at me, and Gabi was completely confused. I could tell by her expression she thought I was nuts.

"What?" I moved my hands to my hips. "I just don't want Lou to go after your soul. You say you want something and he'll try to bargain you for it."

But that wasn't why I was so frantic. Not this time. I didn't want Gabi to wish for something because if she did—it would come true. And not because of Lou. But because I ACCIDENTALLY MADE ALL OF HER WISHES COME TRUE. That's right. *All* of them. It was the only way to explain everything. Why Max was acting all superior, the junk food in her lunch, the automatic A, getting to leave early. Gabi wished for all of those things to happen—and they did.

I couldn't risk her wishing something else—something that could be way, way worse. Especially not with Lou watching.

"I wouldn't take her soul," Lou said.

"No, you'd send Gremory for that," I shot back at him.

"Gremory won't be trying that again. Not after what happened last time."

"What happened?"

"Ahh, that demon," Lou laughed, and shook his head. "Instead of only granting one of his subject's wishes, he accidentally granted them all. What a mess. But that's what happens when you don't have the right training."

Gabi let out a gasp.

Why did she have to pick now to catch on? I glared at her and shook my head ever so slightly. Lou wasn't supposed to see.

But of course he did.

"Angel?" he said.

"What?"

"Have you tried to grant a wish?"

"Of course not." I kept eye contact with him. Looking away would have made me seem guilty.

But Lou wasn't buying it. He was the devil. A pro at spotting deception. "Angel?" he said again.

"Fine," I answered, giving him a half truth. I read in some article that the best way to get away with a lie was to keep it as close to reality as possible. Without too many details. "I haven't granted any wishes, but I'm thinking about it. It'll let me do some good in this world. Unlike you."

"It's too dangerous," he warned me.

"Like having the devil roaming the streets isn't?"

"Let's talk about this." He took a step closer to me.

"No. Now go. I have to get Gabi home. She's sick, remember?"

Without another word, I grabbed Gabi's arm and stormed off, dragging her behind me. She might not have been sick, but something was terribly wrong.

chapter

18

I took Gabi to the McBrin house. It was old and abandoned and we met there every morning so we could walk to school together. No one else ever hung around there. Probably because they were afraid it was haunted.

Gabi was bursting.

"I have powers? This is the absolute coolest thing ever." She looked like a firecracker about to explode. "I wish for—"

"Stop." I was afraid she'd wish for something crazy. Like a pet elephant. "Let's be careful," I instructed. "Why don't you wish for something simple? Like a piece of gum." I had to see if my suspicions were right. If I really messed up the same way as Lou's demon friend.

Gabi closed her eyes and put out her hand. I held

my breath and hoped that I was wrong and that Gabi couldn't make all her secret desires come true.

She opened her eyes and glanced down at her palm. "Nothing there," she moaned. "It didn't work."

I grabbed her hand to see for myself. It was empty. Thank goodness. It was all a mistake. She wasn't responsible for everything that happened in school. "Trust me. This is the best thing that could have happened."

"I guess," Gabi said, smacking a piece of gum between her teeth.

Wait a minute.

"Where did you get that?" I lunged toward her, as if getting a closer look would make the gum disappear. "Where did that gum come from?"

Gabi opened her mouth and the gum dropped out—right into my hand. Which totally would have grossed me out and sent me running to the nearest hand sanitizer if I wasn't freaking out.

"It just appeared. I wished for a piece of gum and there it was." She giggled. "Ha! That just made another piece appear."

"Shhh," I said. "Then don't say anything else. You need to stay quiet. Don't wish for anything else. Don't even think about anything else."

I'd made a Frankenstein! A cuter, skinnier one, with long, light brown hair and perfectly pressed clothes.

But Gabi didn't follow orders very well because all of a sudden a hot fudge sundae appeared in front of her.

"Sorry," she said, licking her lips in anticipation. "I didn't mean to. It just kind of popped in my head. And now here it is."

Gabi eyed the dessert. Then me.

"I wish I had a spoon. And extra whipped cream," she said super fast. One after another the things she wished for appeared. "Sorry, but come on. It's only ice cream. And it looks so good."

"Gabi!" I screamed. "What are you doing? You know how easy it is for wishes to get out of control. You've seen what's happened to me. Something that seems like it won't matter turns into a huge nightmare. What if you accidentally said something like—" I stopped myself. I didn't want to put any ideas in her head. Last thing I needed was for her to repeat some harebrained thing I said, like, "I wish Edward from *Twilight* was my boyfriend." We already had a devil in Goode—the last thing we needed was a coven of vampires. Hot or not.

"Can you please try to reverse what you've done?

Try something small first. We'll work up to the bigger things." Like reversing what she did to Max and figuring out a way get rid of her newfound ability.

"Fine," Gabi said, letting out a big sigh. "I wish the sundae would disappear."

It didn't budge.

"Try actually meaning it," I said.

"I *am* trying," Gabi said.

But I didn't believe her. I saw the look on her face. She was enjoying the power rush. She didn't want it to go away. Sure, maybe some of it, like making Max a Courtney clone, but not the other part. The part that got her ice cream and straight As and who knew what else.

"You have to want to get rid of the sundae. Think of the possibilities. Maybe it's poison."

"A poison sundae?" she said. "Come on."

The shade of ice cream got a little darker, and I dumped it out into the grass before she could take a bite. "See," I screamed. "Did you see that change? One wrong word and you could accidentally kill yourself. DO NOT REPEAT THAT. Gabi, you have to be really careful until I figure out a way to fix this."

"Don't worry," she said, looking way too relaxed for a girl who just had a brush with death by mint chocolate chip. "I'll be careful, and I won't wish for anything crazy. I can handle this. I've seen how you've dealt with your powers. I'll be fine. I promise."

Her reassurance didn't calm me down one bit.

I was in for big trouble. I could feel it.

chapter
✦ 19 ✦

I took a big chug from a bottle of Mom's sweetness serum. I was game for anything that promoted goodness, even one of Mom's concoctions. But it didn't help me solve any of my problems. I was still at a loss about how to undo Gabi's wishes. And I had to hurry. It wouldn't be long before Max made the whole student body his personal butlers. Or . . . Gabi accidentally wished for the end of civilization.

The doorbell distracted me from my thoughts. I tossed the container back in the fridge and made my way into the living room. Mom beat me to the door. "Well, I'm glad to see you are finally learning some manners."

She was talking to Lou. My fists clenched. What did he want? And since when did he bother waiting to be invited in?

"I know you hate it when I pop in unannounced. So I'm working on it."

"Thank you," Mom said. And she sounded like she *actually* appreciated the gesture.

Was Lou trying to use Mom to get to me? Make her all sympathetic to his cause to get to know his daughter? It wasn't going to work. I'd just tell her everything he'd been up to with the soul stealing. Then he'd never be allowed back in.

"Mom," I said, giving Lou a smug look. "Do you know why Lou's really here? What he's been up to recently?" He wasn't going to win this time.

"What are you talking about?" she asked.

"Lou's—"

He cut me off. "Here to help Angel with her pow—"

"NO!" I shouted. Mom didn't know I inherited Lou's evil powers, and I wanted to keep it that way.

"Her what?"

"Her PowerPoint presentation. I suggested she try one for her science project—to give her a leg up on her classmates. I told her I'd help her make it. Isn't that right, Angel? Didn't we say today after school?"

98

Blackmail. That was Lou's plan. Hang out with him or he'd rat me out to my mom. Nicely played. He really was good at this manipulation thing. "Yeah, that's what we said. Let's go."

I slammed my bedroom door shut. "This is not making me like you more."

"You'll come around," he said.

That's what *he* thought. I sat on my bed, put on my iPod, and stuck in the earbuds. So he sat down next to me and plucked them right out. "We need to talk."

I looked up at the ceiling.

"What you said before, about thinking about granting wishes, don't do it."

"Why? Don't like the idea of me helping others?"

"What I don't like," he answered, "is the idea of you doing something that could hurt you."

I ignored him.

"Angel, I'm serious. You don't know what you're doing. Look what happened to Gremory. It was a mess, he thought he was making the man's wish to become a baseball player come true. But his focus wasn't right."

"Yeah, you told me," I said, hoping to end the conversation. "He ended up granting all of the guy's wishes."

"Yes, and that's why I don't want you trying it. It's a very common mistake. Gremory's thoughts were so wrapped up in giving the guy what he wanted that he ended up granting all of the guy's wishes.

"So? It's not like you couldn't reverse it in a millisecond."

"It's not that simple. Once a wish is made it's done. No going back, no altering it. Unless the person who made the wish wants to give it up."

Again Lou was making a big deal out of nothing.

"Okay, if the guy wished for something bad, why wouldn't he want to reverse it?"

"Because," Lou said, "it's all or nothing. The wish was that *all* his wishes would come true. To undo it means giving everything back. Not just the bad stuff. Gremory's subject wanted to be a baseball player way too much to give it up. Sure, there were some things even he would have wanted to reverse. Like when he accidentally wished his coach would shut up, and the guy could no longer speak at all. But nothing was worth giving up his dream."

Then he was a jerk. I wouldn't have that problem with Gabi. She wasn't that baseball player. She wouldn't let someone suffer because of her. She was the nicest, best person in the world. She would definitely give it all up. She wouldn't leave someone silent for the rest of their life or Max all self-absorbed—not even for all the ice-cream sundaes and straight As.

Lou went on with his story, pretending not to notice that I was back to ignoring him. "Gremory, of course, couldn't leave things as they were. And with a little help from me we made the man realize he was better off without wishes. But do you see how dangerous playing around with this power can be? What if the person wished *everyone* would shut up? There would be worldwide ramifications."

"Okay," I said. "You made your point. You can go now. I won't try to grant a wish."

Too bad I already did.

chapter
✦ 20 ✦

I got to the McBrin house extra early the next morning to meet Gabi. Which, if you know me, is super impressive. I am not a morning person at all. But I couldn't sleep. I kept having nightmares that a zombie was after me, wanting me to grant him a wish. Between that and thoughts of Gabi transforming the town into Wonka World, I got my butt in gear extra early. I was there a whole twenty minutes before Gabi showed up.

"Thank God," I said when she finally arrived. "You didn't make any more wishes, did you?"

She said she didn't. But Gabi was the worst liar ever. She looked like she just swallowed a baseball bat, she was that uncomfortable.

"Gabi . . ."

"Okay," she said, and dropped down to the grass.

"I may have made a few itty-bitty ones. But not on purpose. They just happened. And honestly, they're so small, it's like they don't exist at all. I mean, it's nothing to worry about."

"What did you wish for?" I said before she went into a fifty-eight minute oral presentation on why I shouldn't freak out. The girl could talk when she wanted to.

Gabi pulled at her ponytail and twisted the strands around her fingers. "Well, my mom totally doesn't care what I eat anymore or how I do in school." Her voice got higher and faster. "My room has its own dessert bar, a hundred-inch flat screen TV, a whole wall of new books, a water bed, a—" She saw the look on my face and stopped. My jaw was skimming my sneakers.

"Come on," she said, standing back up. "You have to admit it's pretty cool. It didn't hurt anyone. And Rori is sooo jealous. It's awesome." Rori was Gabi's little sister, who was more than a little spoiled—and used to getting whatever she wanted.

"Yeah. Cool until something bad happens. We have to reverse it."

"Too bad we don't know how," she said. The sincerity in her voice was totally fake.

"Good news," I said. "We do." I filled her in on

what Lou had told me about how Gabi had to want to give up her new "power" and relinquish everything she wished for in order to put things back the way they were.

"Everything?" she asked. "I really like the dessert bar in my room."

I put my hands on my hips. "I'll buy you a Twinkies value pack," I promised. "Now please. Before you do something you regret."

"What if I promise to be extra careful?"

"It's too risky."

She knotted her fingers together. "Your powers are risky, too, and you manage."

"It's not the same thing. You just have to say or think something and poof, it's here. I have to have perfect concentration to make anything go right. My passing thoughts don't make things appear out of thin air." I took an extra long pause for dramatic effect. "Do it for Max. Do it for all the people he's bossing around and turning into his servants. Do it for me."

My little guilt trip worked. Gabi nodded. "Fine."

"Just clear your mind and focus on how you don't want wishes."

I watched her. It seemed like she was concentrating. Her eyes were squeezed closed and it looked like she was holding her breath. "Okay," I said when she opened her eyes. "Try to make a wish."

"I wish for a diamond—" She paused when she looked at me.

Way to think small, I thought.

"Bracelet," Gabi finished.

And the shimmering jewels appeared encrusted around Gabi's wrist.

"Whoa," she said, her face almost as bright as the bracelet.

The reversal hadn't worked. Gabi was still as magical as before. What went wrong? I watched her hold the jewels up to the light. She looked relieved. "Gabi," I said. "You have to want to give the wishes back for it to work."

"But what if I don't really want to?" she asked.

"Then you're dooming Max to be all Courtney-esque for the rest of his life, for everyone in school to worship him for eternity, and for me to who knows what. All because you want a few wishes. It's totally selfish."

She dropped her head. "You're right," she conceded. "I can do this. I wish I could undo everything. I don't want wishes."

I hoped that was enough. "Test it."

"I wish I had a matching diamond necklace," she said, her voice sounding the tiniest bit hopeful.

Her neck went from having nothing on it to being covered in jewels.

Trying to give back the wishes didn't work.

Gabi obviously wanted them, and I had no clue how to change that.

chapter
✧ 21 ✧

"I thought you said you'd give up the wishes," I said, throwing my arms up in the air.

"I tried," Gabi said. "Really!" she added when she saw the look I was giving her. "But it's not my fault if way down deep I want to keep them. How am I supposed to control that?"

"Maybe by thinking about the harm your wishes have caused?! That should make you want to give them up."

Gabi scrunched up her nose. "What harm?"

"Max for one. All the name-calling and pushing people around. How do you think his parents are going to feel when they realize their son has turned into a monster?"

Gabi shrugged her shoulders. "I guess I don't think it's so bad. Courtney's the same way, and she seems pretty happy. She gets whatever she wants."

Sounds like someone else I know. "Then what about

the danger?" I asked. "If you accidentally wish for the wrong thing? Something really, really bad. Then what?"

She gave me a half smile. "I just don't think that will happen."

I didn't even know what to say.

"Sorry," she said. "I can't help wanting what I secretly want. I'd give up the wishes if I could."

She left me with no choice. It was time for a different approach. A powerful one.

"I hope you mean that," I said, "because I think I know what will work."

Gabi backed up a step. "I know you, Angel. Don't get any big ideas. I'm not your guinea pig."

She really did know me well. She knew exactly what I was going to do. I would use my powers on her—the strongest stuff I could muster. "You didn't have a problem with me using 'my gift' on you before. You even volunteered. It was your idea for me to grant you a wish in the first place."

"That's different," she said, moving back some more. "Giving something is a lot easier than taking it away. Besides, this wish stuff has you totally freaked out. And when that happens, your powers never work right."

I took a step toward her. "I'm perfectly calm," I said, although my heart was racing faster than usual.

"What do you want to do?"

"It's easy." I smiled, showing off my dimples. I wanted to her to feel reassured, even though I was nervous. "I'm just going to take away the wishes."

She shook her head. "You tried yesterday, and it didn't work."

"Yesterday, I didn't know what I was up against. I only tried to undo part of the wish—Max being all evil. I didn't know I had to try to take away everything you wished for."

"Didn't Lou say the only way this could be reversed was for the wish maker to want to give it all up? That was there was no other way?"

"Lou says a lot of things that aren't true. Of course there's another way. My powers gave you the wishes; they have to be able to take them away. Lou just doesn't want me trying anything advanced without his guidance. He's hoping I'll come beg him to start my lessons up again." I put my hand on her arm. "Let's just give it a try. I can do it."

She moved away. "You're making me nervous."

"Don't be."

"You have that look," Gabi said. "The one Rori gets

before she does something stupid. Like that time she skateboarded down the staircase and broke her leg."

"Please, Gabi, what can it hurt to try?"

"I don't even want to think about that," she answered.

"Come on. You said before that you were willing to give up the wishes. But something deep down wasn't letting you. Well, if we use my powers to get rid of them, it doesn't matter what you want deep down."

She dropped down onto the grass and picked at a dandelion. "Fine. It's not like I have much choice. You're going to do it, anyway."

That was true. I sat across from her. "Just relax," I said. "And think about the wishes while I focus on taking them away." I put my hands on her head. "Undo the wishes. I wish they'd disappear. Make them disappear. Make them disappear."

I tried to send out energy from my fingertips to Gabi, zapping the original wish—that all of her wishes would come true—away. I visualized her thinking about it in her mind. I pictured it vanishing. *I want it gone. I want it gone. I want it gone.*

I felt something like an energy bolt surge through me. It was the feeling of success.

"I think I did it," I told Gabi, moving my hands from her head. "Wish for something."

"I wish you weren't a nutcase."

"Ha-ha." I stood up. "Your wishes don't work on me. Wish for something real."

"Fine. I wish the windows on the McBrin house weren't boarded up."

I almost fell backward as I watched the wood paneling remove itself. How was it possible? "I was so sure I made it disappear."

Gabi's phone rang, and she picked it up. Within seconds her whole face was drained of color. When she hung up she stared at me.

"That was my mom," she said, her voice so low and hollow it gave me goose bumps. "I think you may have made something else disappear. My sister is gone."

chapter

✦ 22 ✦

"It's impossible," I said. "I didn't make your sister go anywhere."

"Then where is she?" Gabi shrieked.

"She's probably just acting up to get some attention." I chewed on three of my nails at once. *Please don't let me be the cause.*

"My mom said Rori disappeared right in front of her eyes. That one second she was there, the next she wasn't. That had to be your doing."

She was right. "I know, just wish for her back!"

"I wish Rori was here, standing right in front of me," Gabi said.

Nothing happened. It looked like Gabi couldn't undo my mistakes.

Gabi was clawing at her arms. She was panicked. "How did this happen?"

"I don't know. Were you thinking about her when I was trying to undo the wish?"

"No. Yes. Maybe. I don't know. My mind might have flashed to how happy she'd be now that my wishes were gone. But what does that matter?"

Because it meant I messed up royally. Instead of taking away Gabi's wishes, I took away something else she was thinking about.

I had never seen Gabi look like this. So . . . so . . . desperate. It was like I slapped all the joy out of her.

"Well," I said. "It wasn't like you liked your sister that much, anyway."

Gabi looked at me like I was crazy. "She can be a pain, but she's still my sister! I would never want her to disappear. Not for good!"

"She didn't," I told her. "This is nothing. I'll get her back. I'll use my powers. I just need to think for a minute." I paced back and forth and took a few deep breaths. *In and out. In and out.* I was going to bring Rori back. Bring Rori back. Bring Rori back. I was going to bring Rori back right now.

A giant roar, followed by a scream, brought me out of my relaxation trance.

Standing face-to-face with Gabi was a lion.

She took a step backward, and the lion followed

suit. "Get rid of it," she whisper-shouted through clenched teeth.

Get rid of it? I didn't even know how I got it there in the first place. The animal lunged right for my best friend. "No!" I screamed, and closed my eyes as hard as I could. I couldn't watch. My best friend was about to be lion food. It was official. I was definitely evil. Gabi's life was over because of me. How was I going to go on? When I opened my eyes, Gabi was gone. Had the lion pulverized her? Where was she?

"Gabi," I yelled. "Gabi!" I squeezed my eyes shut again to keep the tears from streaming out. It didn't work. They came, anyway. But this time when I opened them up again, Gabi was back.

What was going on?

She raced to my side and clutched onto me, and I held her just as tight. "Where did you go?" I asked her.

"I don't know. One second I was there, then the next I just disappeared."

It was me! My powers. They did something right! They took Gabi out of danger. But it wasn't exactly time for a celebration. I had a hungry lion standing right in front of me roaring its head off.

Roaring! That was it. Instead of bringing *Rori* back,

I brought back a *roar*ing lion. It was like for every one thing that went right with my powers another zillion went wrong.

"Do something," Gabi said.

"Go back where you came from," I said. "Send the roaring lion back." I said it, I thought it, I breathed in and out, I tried to will it away. And finally in a poof, the lion was gone.

"You could have killed us!" Gabi said, stepping back from me.

That would definitely have sent my soul straight to the underworld. Intentionally or not, it was like I was destined to do horrible things.

"Angel, are you even listening to me?" Gabi screamed. "We need to get Rori back."

"Sorry," I said, snapping back from my thoughts. "You're right. It will work this time. I'm sure of it. Bring back Gabi's sister, Rori. Bring back Gabi's sister. Bring back Gabi's sister."

I shouted it out as loud as I could, closed my eyes, and even made a rhyme. "Powers don't fail me, it's Gabi's sister we want to see. It is her that we miss, please bring us Gabi's sis."

Nothing.

I closed my eyes and pictured seeing Gabi hugging

115

her sister. "Please bring back Gabi's sister," I whispered into the air.

And then finally, from a twenty-foot distance, I saw the silhouette of a little girl materialize.

"Where am I?" she asked. Yes! I did it! I brought her back!

At least I thought I did.

But then I looked closer. It wasn't Rori. It was some other little girl. A little girl who looked terrified. "Where's my sister?" she asked.

"What?" I asked.

"Where's Gabi?" Panic rose in her voice. "She was just here."

Just perfect. I brought Gabi's sister here all right. I just got the wrong Gabi.

"Don't worry," I told her. "You're okay."

She looked at me like I was a boogeyman who terrorized small defenseless children in their sleep and cut off their thumbs for souvenirs. She wasn't that far off. I *was* the spawn of the devil.

"We'll call your sister," Gabi said. "What's the number?"

The girl looked hesitant, but gave us the info. "Wait," I said to Gabi. "Block your number. The last thing we need is her sister tracking us down."

Gabi gave me a look before she dialed. I knew what it meant. It meant I was way too good at this whole deception business. That maybe I did take after my dad.

I tried not to think about that. I couldn't. Not now. First I had to concentrate on sending the girl back to her sister. Then I could deal with my messed-up lineage.

"Hello," Gabi said into the phone.

"Hello," the other Gabi said so loud I could hear from where I was standing. "Susie, is that you?"

"She's okay," my Gabi said.

"Who is this? Where's my sister? I'm calling the police."

NO! She couldn't do that. I needed to get her sister back now.

"There you are. Thank God. Susie, where were—" the phone line went dead. Gabi—one of them—disconnected the call.

"You did it," Gabi said. "You sent her back."

My powers tended to be more active when I was panicked out of my mind. And the idea of getting charged with kidnapping certainly ranked up there in the crisis zone.

"And I'll get Rori back, too."

117

"I knew I never should have let you try to undo my wish. I can't believe this is happening."

"I'm so sorry. I want to put everything back to normal. I'm trying." I coughed back a sniffle. My best friend was going to hate me forever if I didn't fix this. *Pleeeaaaasseeee!!!* I begged my powers. *Please work. Please bring back Gabi Gottlieb's sister, Rori. Right now!*

"Rori!" Gabi cried out.

Finally! There was Rori standing right in front of us! I guess my panic and prayers paid off. Thank goodness.

"What? Where . . . How did I get here?" Rori was clearly confused.

Gabi did a one-eighty. She went from down in the dumps to all smiles. She was practically bouncing. "I wish Rori was back with my mother and that neither of them remember that she ever went missing."

And just like that Rori was gone.

Gabi dialed her Mom. "Is Rori there? She wasn't missing at all? No reason. Okay. Bye." She turned to me. "Everything's fine. They don't remember a thing about her disappearance. How about that? It looks like I've got this power thing down. Nothing to worry about."

"It's harder than it looks," I warned her. "Did you see the kind of bad that can happen? Disappearing sisters!"

"That was you. Not me."

"This time." I shook my head. "You're going to have to try harder to give back the wishes."

I didn't want to think what would happen if she didn't.

chapter
✦ 23 ✦

"Well, if it isn't the loser brigade," Courtney called out from the school steps as Gabi and I approached.

Her groupies, Jaydin and Lana, of course broke into a fit of laughter. "The only problem," Jaydin said through her giggles, "is that I can't tell which one takes the prize. The freak show or the blabbermouth."

"That's a tough one," Lana chimed in. "You can't even go on looks. They're both pretty horrendous. Double-A's fire-red hair is practically blinding me. And Gabi's is so mousy that it gives me the shivers."

"Yeah," Courtney said. "Where do you cut your hair? The . . ."—The smirk on her face was replaced by a sweet smile. In fact, Courtney's whole stance changed. She dropped her hands from her hips and crossed them in front of her. Her voice even got softer—". . . the beauty shop on Goode Street? They do the best blowouts. My mom always goes there."

Okay? What was going on? Was this a trap? "No," I said.

"Well," Courtney said. "If you ever want to check it out, just let me know. We can make it a day of beauty!"

"And we can all give one another manicures after," Jaydin chirped in. "It'll be so much fun, and I have the perfect color for you, Gabi. It will go amazing with your skin tone."

Since when did they want me *or* Gabi around?

This was weird. Then I had my duh moment. It wasn't weird. It was the "work" of my best friend.

I turned to Gabi. "What did you do?"

"Well," she whispered, and tugged at her ponytail, "when they were insulting us it's possible a couple of thoughts may have crossed through my mind. And I may have wished that they'd be nice. Like really, majorly, super nice."

Okay. It could have been worse. Like what went through my mind. That they'd turn into bugs that I could squash with one of Courtney's designer shoes. So I guess nice was nothing in comparison.

"Gabi," Jaydin said, rushing toward her. "Can I

help you with your bag? It looks really heavy, and I don't want you to hurt your back."

"I'll take it," Lana said. "I'm stronger, and I don't want you to get hurt either, Jaydin."

"Girls," Courtney said, flashing her teeth at me in a big, old smile. "Don't forget about Angel. Do you need any help with anything? Just let us know. Nothing makes us happier than doing things for others."

This reminded me of one of those body snatcher movies. Courtney and Co. had been replaced by pods. They were totally all smiles and good deeds. It was eerie. I mean, they deserved a lesson—for someone to get back at them for all the hurt and cruelty they'd brought on—but this much niceness was pretty sickening.

They were way over the top, fawning all over us and anyone who walked by. It was a little repulsive. But Gabi actually looked pleased with herself.

"Please, let me take the bag," Lana begged Gabi. "It makes me so sad when I can't help others."

"Uh, okay," Gabi said, and handed her bag to the pod people.

"I'll get this right to your homeroom," Lana said, nodding furiously. She began running, but stopped herself. She turned around. "I better not run. Running can cause accidents. And accidents aren't nice."

Gabi snorted. I smacked her arm. This was not funny. Okay, maybe a little. But it was also something that needed to be fixed immediately.

"Angel!" Courtney shook her finger at me. "We don't hit friends. That's not nice."

Then she saw D.L., who was making his way up the stairs. "It's so good to see you," she said, giving him a huge hug. "And don't you look *nice!*"

That word was starting to give me a nervous tic.

D.L. pushed her away. "What is *with* you? One day you don't even want to be around me and the next day you're syrupy sweet."

She grinned at him. "I'm sorry. Did I do something to upset you? I'll make it up to you. Would you like me to write you a letter and apologize? There's nothing like a note from the heart."

He just stared back at her. "Okay. Who are you? What did you do with Courtney?"

She slapped her hand lightly on his chest. "You're so silly."

"Max," Jaydin called out, waving to the school's new king. "I did all of the math homework. Just come to me whenever you need help."

He didn't even stop and acknowledge her.

Instead, he just walked into school, a posse of people by his side.

Now not only did I have to deal with Mad Max, but I had Courteous Courtney and Company. And who knew what was in store next? There was one thing I did know—this was getting way out of hand. And I needed to do something about it.

"You know what we should do?" Jaydin said to Courtney. "Something nice for Max. I bet the home ec room is open. Let's go make him some cookies."

Courtney clapped her hands together. "That's such a good idea, Jaydin. You are so smart. And pretty, too. See you later, D.L. We're going to go make some cookies. You can come. You too, Angel and Gabi. We would never want to exclude anyone from our group."

Yeah, right.

D.L. gave me a look. Almost like I had something to do with what was going on with his girlfriend.

I just shrugged.

He couldn't pin any of this on me. But it was probably only a matter of time before he, or someone else, could.

These wishes needed to stop before Gabi got us in big trouble.

chapter 24

The lockers turned a light shade of lavender and the walls a deep purple as we headed to homeroom.

"Gabi!"

"Sorry! I was just thinking about how they'd be so much prettier if they weren't that drab green. And it just happened. Besides," she said, "I don't know why you're getting so worked up. Big deal if the walls are purple. It makes the school look better. How is that a bad thing?"

Before I could respond, I noticed Cole heading toward us.

"There you are. I've been looking all over for you," he said.

He looked so cute. His hair was getting longer and some of his curls flopped right over his eyes.

When he tossed his head to move them away, I'm pretty sure my stomach did a back handspring.

"You guys are so lucky you got out of that test yesterday," Cole said. "It was awful. Mrs. Torin expected us to remember every single little thing that happened in the play. Which was impossible. I read the thing twice, and I still barely understood any of it. I can't wait until we're done with Shakespeare."

"It should be soon," I told him. "I think she's going to have us write our own plays next. Maybe we can all work on one together."

"You know, I was thinking," he said, rocking back on his feet, "that maybe . . ."

Gabi started to wander off. "Gabi, wait up. Hold on, Cole." I wanted to talk to Cole, but I *needed* to talk to Gabi. To warn her to watch what she said and thought. "I'm sorry," I told Cole, "but can I catch up with you in class? There's something really important I need to tell Gabi."

I hated sending him away, especially when he seemed so excited to see me, but this was mega important. I needed to shake some sense into Gabi before she made another wish.

Cole looked from Gabi to me and back again. Then he nodded and walked off. He looked so disappointed.

And while this may sound awful, it actually made me feel happy. It meant he really, truly liked me. Which was good, because I really, truly liked him, too.

Once the coast was clear, I turned my attention back to Gabi, who was sipping from a can of soda. "Where'd you get that?"

"I was thirsty."

"And you wished for it on purpose!"

She didn't answer.

"Gabi, you can't go around making wishes."

"Why not?"

Why not? Was she losing her mind? Were the wishes interfering with her brain waves and causing her to lose all sense of reason? "Because one day the wrong wish is going to come true!"

"Me having a soda is not going to cause the school to collapse. I'm not going to wish for anything like that."

I cringed as she spoke, half expecting the walls to come caving in. "But if you word something wrong, who knows what will happen? Try and reverse the wish making. Now."

"No," she said, shaking her head.

"Gabi, you said you would." I crossed my arms over my chest. I needed to hold in the gloom and dread before it oozed out of my pores and contaminated the whole school.

"No. You did."

"Fine. Do you want me to try and reverse it again?"

"Are you kidding? I'm not risking that. What if the same thing happens as before? And you make Rori disappear and next time you can't get her back. Besides"—she shrugged her shoulders—"the wishes are kind of fun."

"But they're dangerous."

"I can handle powers. You're the one who should come with a warning label. Not me."

She did not *just say that!* "Gabi!"

"What? It's true."

I was afraid if I spoke, flames would come flying out of my mouth. How *dare* she! Okay, yes. My powers weren't perfect, and I've been known to have technical difficulties surrounding them. But I was getting so much better. My powers had barely gone off on their own at all since the dance. Well, unless you counted when I saved Gabi from getting eaten by a lion. But that was a good thing.

"Think about it," she went on. "This is the best scenario ever. Now we're both special. We can do amazing things." She headed off to class with me on her tail.

I had to make her understand. "You don't need powers to do amazing things."

Gabi stopped right in front of a corkboard with pictures from the school musical *You're a Good Man, Charlie Brown* pinned to it. "No. You don't need them. But they sure can help."

She eyed a picture of Courtney as Lucy. The part she was up for but didn't get. Her finger traced the border of the photo. "I really did like being the assistant director. But it would have been fun to be the star."

"Gabi, let's go," I said. "Whatever you're thinking—don't."

I managed to peel her away from the photos.

"Don't hate me," she said. "I didn't mean to do it. Honest."

"Do what?"

"You're about to see."

chapter 25

"There she is," a woman at the end of the hall said, and pointed at Gabi. Then she raced over to us, followed by a big guy holding a video camera. And there were even more people with cameras following him.

The commotion got everyone's attention. I wouldn't have been surprised if the whole school was jammed into that hallway trying to figure out what was going on. Which I was pretty curious about myself.

"Who is she?" I asked Gabi.

The woman answered for her. "I'm Elena, the producer of a new reality show where we turn regular middle school kids into stars. And our first episode will feature Goode's very own Gabi Gottlieb."

That's what Gabi wished for? To be a star! And of a reality show no less! Yuck.

"Tell us what you think, Gabi," Elena said, shoving a microphone in her face.

"I think it's pretty awesome!"

Personally, I thought it stunk. A reality show meant cameras would be following Gabi everywhere. How was I supposed to talk any sense into her when everything I said would be recorded for all of America to hear?

"Great, and how about the rest of you?" The main cameraman turned and panned the hallway to get everyone's expressions, which pretty much consisted of awe, excitement, surprise, and wonder. Well, all except D.L. He covered his face with his arm and said, "I'm out of here. This school is messed up. I'm not going to be on some stupid reality show." Then he bolted. We were actually on the same page for a change. I didn't want be a part of it, either.

Max had the opposite reaction. He bullied his way toward Elena. "You have the wrong person," he said. "The only one with star quality at this school is me."

"Actually," Elena said, "Gabi's our girl. I've never seen someone with so much star power."

"What about me?" he asked.

"Sorry," she said. "If you're not a part of Gabi's life, you're not a part of the show."

131

Mighty Max looked stunned that someone didn't gush all over him. But Elena wasn't under the Max spell like everyone else. So she didn't care what one snot nose eighth-grader thought.

"Speaking of which"—Elena turned to Gabi—"we're going to want to interview the people closest to you. Keep our eye on them as well."

"First there's Angel." Gabi pointed to me. "She's my very best friend. And Cole sits with us at lunch. Oh, and I have a secret admirer, too. I'm not positive who it is yet, but I do have a guess."

She scanned the room, probably searching for Marc to see if he'd let on that he was the guy crushing on her.

"Great," Elena said, motioning to one of the cameramen. "Let's start with the best friend." Next she addressed me. "Since you seem to know Gabi the best, we're going to devote one cameraman specifically to you. That way we catch anything you say about her even when she's not around. So just be natural. After an hour you'll forget you're even being filmed."

No way was I letting a camera follow me around. It was bad enough Gabi didn't seem to mind having one on her.

"I'm going to start by asking you a few questions," Elena said.

I stepped away. I've seen enough reality shows to know the truth. She got paid to torture teens—to make their lives miserable and air it on national television. It wouldn't surprise me if reality TV was invented by Lou.

Lou!

What if he popped in to spy on me when the cameras were rolling? How would I explain a man appearing out of nowhere?! Elena would totally try to uncover my secret. Or worse. Lou would realize she was onto us and banish her to the underworld. I couldn't let that happen. I was not going to be responsible for anything bad happening to anyone.

"Thanks," I told her. "But I'm not going to be on the show."

"We need you," she pressed. "You're Gabi's best friend."

"Sorry." I walked away, but they followed me. "I said I'm not doing the show."

"I heard you," Elena said. "But like it or not, you are a part of this."

What was *with* this woman? "If you don't leave me alone, I'll call the police. I'm underage, and you can't film me without permission." Ha. So there, I showed her. You couldn't go around filming minors. In school!

"Actually," Elena said, "I can." She pulled out a stack of papers. "I have permission slips signed by the guardian of every student here. Including yours."

What?! No way my mom would sign something like that. She thinks TV in general is sinful. But reality TV? She thinks that is more disgusting than the sludge forming near the sewer. She says it brings out the worst in people—entertainment at the expense of people's feelings. "Prove it," I said.

"Last name?" Elena asked.

"Garrett."

She rifled through her bag, and then she pulled it right out. A piece of paper containing Tammi Garrett's curlicue signature, complete with a yin-yang symbol dotting the *i*. It was definitely not a forgery.

Gabi's wish covered everything down to the last minute detail. Even the permission slips. Maybe she was better at this power thing than I was.

Wait. No she wasn't. She was the one who made a whole camera crew appear at school. I may not have mastered my gift, but I didn't go around making crazy wishes.

The late bell went off, and Elena turned to one of the camera guys. "You, stay with the best friend. We're going to get Gabi walking into class."

Gabi had a ginormous grin on her face as she moved down the hall. And there was a whole group of people clamoring around her. Even Cole. Everyone seemed to think this show was super exciting.

I, on the other hand, was pretty sure I had a look of dread on my face. Not that I knew for sure. But I was bound to find out eventually. The camera guy was recording every move I made. This was going to have to stop pronto. What if my powers accidentally went off? I couldn't chance it.

"Max," I yelled out. "This guy wants to interview you."

Mr. Big Shot couldn't resist the call of the camera—even if I was the one paging him. So he came racing over.

"Sorry, son," the camera guy said. "I need to follow her. Not you."

"He's much more interesting than I am," I said, slipping behind Max.

"Definitely true," Max agreed. And while he had the cameraman cornered, I made my escape. I just needed to be one of the crowd.

I was not going to be exposed as the devil's daughter on national television!

chapter
✦ 26 ✦

"Why so sad, Angel?" Courtney asked, skipping over to me in science class.

"Shh." I glanced up at her from behind my textbook. I was hiding behind it to keep the camera guy from spotting me.

"Have a cookie," she said, her voice extra chipper. "Cookies make everything better."

I highly doubted it. A cookie wasn't going to fix anything. Not the wishes Gabi made, the fact that I hadn't succeeded in doing any good deeds, or that I hadn't been able to get near Gabi all day. Not without a camera crew and a whole slew of people standing by. I didn't even try and sit next to her in class. That was just asking for unwanted attention. Max, on the other hand, jumped at the opportunity. He was kissing up to Gabi nonstop. He even insisted that he got the seat next to her. And since Miss Simmons thought Max was the greatest, he got want he wanted.

"You can have two," Courtney continued, handing me her baked goods.

"Cut it out," I said, pushing her arm away and causing her to drop the cookies on the ground.

"Oh my," she said. "Now we can't leave a mess, can we? Don't you worry, I'll take care of that right now."

She bent down to pick it up, and I grabbed her shoulders. "Snap out of it. You should be biting my head off." Was I nuts? I actually wanted Courtney to insult me? "Don't you think I deserve to eat the cookies off the ground? Because I'm no better than a cockroach. Or something. Come on, you're better at this than I am. Say something mean, do something."

"I . . .wha . . . I . . ." Courtney sat down in a chair, her hands grasped behind her neck. "I could never say anything like that. That's just not nice." She put her head down on the desk. Apparently this Courtney couldn't even handle hearing mean things.

I looked up. My attempt to dodge the camera guy hadn't worked at all. He had been rolling the whole time. They were going to make me look like a psycho on national television and Courtney the sweetest

137

girl ever. But that was the least of my problems. Who cared if everyone thought I was crazy. . . .

That was the answer! That's how I could talk to Gabi. In a crazy code. Anyone who was listening would just think I was strange, but she'd know what I meant.

I marched right over to Gabi. "Can I talk to you?"

She looked at the clock. We still had a little time before the bell went off. "Of course," she said.

I could almost feel the camera zooming in on me. I used my hand to shield my face. "Gabi, you've taken this too darn far. Enough is enough. We need to . . . undo . . . the . . ." I couldn't think of anything. *What do we need to undo? What do we need to undo?* "We need to undo the . . . *sweater!*" It was the best I could do.

"Huh?" she asked.

"You know. The *sweater.*" I bugged my eyes out at her. "The one we tried to knit. There's a big mistake in it. We need to undo it now. If we keep going forward with it, it's just going to be harder to fix later."

"You're making a big deal out of nothing," Gabi said, catching on. "The *sweater* is fine. You're the only one who even notices a problem. Everyone else thinks it's great. Me included."

I needed her onboard. If she refused to give back the wishes, there was nothing I could do. The reversal wouldn't work without her. "It's not great. It's seriously flawed and bound to get worse. I wouldn't want to be a part of something bad. Especially with my history."

"You won't be. Not if I'm super careful as I move forward. Just because your dad is an awful knitter doesn't mean we can't make awesome sweaters with the wool you got from him. I'll—"

The bell cut her off.

"Everyone back in their seats," Miss Simmons called out.

"I wish I could have a minute to talk to Angel," Gabi answered.

"Not a problem," the teacher answered. "Take a minute to talk."

"See." Gabi gave me a big smile. She thought making Miss Simmons do what she wanted was cool. But controlling people—their thoughts, their actions— it wasn't right. It was something the devil would do. "Everything is under control."

"It's not. Don't you understand? You can't make people . . ." Shoot. The cameras. "Umm, you can't make people wear a sweater they don't want to wear. They should have the choice. But this wouldn't even

139

be an issue if you'd just agree to undo it. Make it so wearing it isn't an option."

"Sorry." She seemed to be saying that quite a bit.

"Okay, everyone to your seats," Miss Simmons said.

Gabi's nose scrunched up. "I said I wanted a minute."

"Guess your *minute* is up." Every word counted when you used your powers. That was something I knew from experience.

"Well, I wish I had the whole class to do what I wanted," Gabi said.

On cue, Miss Simmons announced we had a free period.

"Gabi, stop!" I told her.

But she didn't care what I had to say. Obviously. Because a second later, some guy was carrying in a massage chair for her. I just leaned against the desk and glared at her. She pretended not to notice. She was having too much fun. A total power rush. Elena took the opportunity to go over plans for the reality show. Apparently as part of the show they were going to link Gabi to celebrities, have her go to great parties where she'd have her photo taken, and all sorts of things to convince people she was a rising star.

"What do you think of Mara's Daughters?" Gabi asked her. "They're my absolute favorite band ever. Any chance we can get them?"

"We can definitely have them on the show," Elena said.

"That would be awesome," Gabi shrieked. "I listen to them all the time. I wish I could hear them now."

I wasn't sure if she did that on purpose or not, but I was ready. As soon as the word *wish* came out of her mouth, I was on my feet ready to pounce. And it was a good thing, too, because just then the sound of a drumbeat came from the hallway. Booking it as fast as I could, I ran out the door, slamming it shut behind me.

I didn't know what to deal with first. The fact that the coolest band in the whole world, Mara's Daughters, was playing in the halls of Goode Middle School with no clue how they got there. (This noise would inevitably disrupt the other classes.) Or the cameraman that was no doubt making his way to the hallway to see what I was up to.

"Stop playing," I ordered the band as I smushed my back up against the classroom door. No way was I letting the cameraman out here. But just as I suspected, he was trying to follow me. I could feel the door and myself starting to move. The guy was a lot stronger than I was. There was no choice. With a wave of my arm, I gestured for the door to close. I couldn't help but smile a little as it swung back shut. At least I still could control some of my powers.

With my arm out, I held it closed, but I couldn't stay like that forever. There were too many other things to focus on. So I moved the drumstick from the hand of Beleth, the drummer, to the space between the bottom of the door and the floor, jamming it closed.

"What?" Beleth asked, staring at the drumstick.

"Don't panic," I told her and her twin sisters, Vale and Vinea. "I can explain everything. What you just saw, how you got here, everything." And I was going to just as soon as I could come up with something that didn't sound insane. "Umm, you see," I said, looking up for some divine inspiration. "It's just that, well, it's actually kind of funny. I—"

Vale let out a giggle. "Relax, Angel. We know about your pow—"

"Don't tell her to relax," Vinea interrupted. "She can't just go around summoning us." Vale glared at me with a look that made my skin prickle.

"Watch it," Beleth warned. "Mess with her, you mess with *him*."

Vinea seemed to know exactly what that meant,

but I didn't. What were they talking about? Did they know who I was? Who my father was? I was suddenly very afraid. Did Gabi do something? Did she wish that the world knew my secret?

Vale put her hands out in front of her. "Ignore Vinea. She can be a beast when she doesn't get enough sleep. But don't worry. She's not going to hurt you."

Now it was my turn to ask the questions. "What's going on?" I whispered.

"Angel," she said, smiling. "You're not the only one with a secret."

It took me a moment to comprehend what she said. "Excuse me?!"

"You're not the only one who can *do* things."

My eyes opened so wide, I thought they were going to fall out of their sockets and roll away. Did they have special powers, too? No, I reasoned with myself. They couldn't. Although, it would explain why they didn't flip out when I used my powers. "What kind of things?" I asked cautiously.

Vinea moved her arm and sent me flying against the locker. "That kind of thing," she said, smirking. "We're like you."

"Oh my God," I said.

"Not so much Him," Vinea said. "We're more underworld type of girls."

No way. They were like me?! "Are you guys the devil's daughters, too?"

All three of them burst out laughing. "Of course not," Vale said. "We're demons."

"*You?*" I took a step away from them. Was my favorite band evil? Was their music their way of luring people to the dark side?

Vinea scrunched up her nose. "For Lucifer's daughter, you're pretty clueless about the workings of the underworld. How could you not have heard of Mara?"

Vale hit her twin on the arm. "Give her a break. You know she grew up *up here*."

Vinea rolled her eyes at her sister. "She should know these things." Then she put her focus on me. "Our dad is Mara. A pretty *major* demon."

"It's okay," Beleth said, pushing her long, dark hair behind her ear, her signature silver bangles jingling with the movement. "You can relax." I hadn't even realized that I had put about twenty feet between us. "Really. You're safe. We're the same band you met on your birthday."

The band played a concert in Goode the night of

my thirteenth birthday. "I had no idea you were . . . you know."

"It never even crossed your mind?" Vinea asked. "Not even after we called you up to join us onstage at our concert and called you by name? I mean, we even sang happy birthday to you."

I bit my pinky nail. "I thought it was my dad's doing."

Vale nodded. "He *was* responsible for it happening, but we were in on it. Our father owed him a favor. He said he'd call it even if we played a concert in Goode for you."

Did they work for my father? I put my arm out, ready to send them flying if I had to. Who knew what plans they had for me? You couldn't trust someone from the underworld.

"Calm down," Vinea said. "I'm sure we're not the first demons you've met. You probably see them all the time. Well, in addition to your dad, who's sort of like head demon. Tons of them prefer living on Earth."

"Tons?" Whoa. This was a major mind trip. Was evil all around me? Were there demons lurking around school, just waiting for Lou's orders to take some souls?

"Not tons," Beleth said, then glared at Vinea. "You're scaring her."

"Scaring *her*? We're the ones who should be scared. *She's* the devil's daughter."

I ignored her last remark. "You're demons? Does that mean you're evil?"

Vinea raised her eyebrow at me. "Not anymore."

Huh?! "What's that supposed to me—"

Beleth cut me off. "We're the same people you met before. Not all demons are bad."

"Really?"

"Give us a break," Vinea said, rolling her eyes. "You're kind of like a demon, too. Well, half demon. And are you bad? No. And neither are we." I lowered my arms. Maybe they were in the same situation as me. Which meant it was possible to come from the underworld and still be good. It was the one decent piece of information I'd heard in days.

"Now did you want something?" Beleth asked. "Why did you summon us here?"

"Huh? Oh!" They thought I had called them.

"It *was* you, wasn't it?" she said.

"Of course it was her," Vinea interrupted. "Who else in Goode would summon us?"

I decided not to tell them about Gabi. They might

not be so understanding if they realized they were called by a mere human on a wish-making kick. And who knew, maybe Vale was a huge gossip. Then the whole underworld would know about Gabi in an instant—including Lou. And I had enough to deal with without adding him to the mix.

"You know what," I said, staring at the cuff of my jeans. "I don't even remember why I called you here. You can just go. Sorry to bug you guys. But thanks for coming." I gave a little wave.

"What?" Vinea asked.

"This whole demon thing made me forget why I called you here," I lied because I didn't know what else to say.

"Whatever," she said.

And poof, they were gone. But just as fast they were back.

"What now?" Vinea asked.

"What do you mean?" I asked.

"You just summoned us again."

"No I di—" I didn't, but Gabi's wish did. The band would probably keep getting the call until the wish was granted. How was I supposed to get around that? There had to be a way. I racked my brain.

The wording of the wish! I could get around it that

way. The same way D.L. didn't fawn all over Max because he was absent when Gabi wished everyone *in* school would adore him, and how Simmons gave us just *one* minute to talk. "Just hold on a second, okay?" I told the band.

I ran over to my locker and pulled out my Mara's Daughters CD. Max had given it to me on my birthday, back before he was mean. "Okay," I said, racing back to them. "Just give me a minute and then you can leave again, and I won't call you back." *Hopefully,* I said to myself.

"Why did you call us in the first place?" Beleth asked.

Oh right. I had to tell them something. "For this," I said holding out the CD. "I was hoping you could all sign it for me."

"You called us here, not knowing we were demons, risking your secret, for autographs?" Vinea questioned me.

It did sound stupid, but it wasn't like I had a lot of time to come up with a better explanation. I just needed them gone before they figured out what was really going on and told my father. "I'm a really big fan."

"Obviously," Vinea said, grabbing the CD from

my hand. They all scrawled their signatures on it and handed it back.

"Count to sixty and then you can go," I told them.

I didn't wait to hear what they said. I flung the drumstick out of the door and bolted back into class, straight to the computer station. I stuffed the CD into the drive closest to me and hit play. The first song on the disc filled the room.

"What's going on?" Elena asked.

"Nothing." I made my way back to the door. I peered under the shade on the window just in time to watch Mara's Daughters disappear.

My whole body froze when I saw Beleth return. But she didn't stay long. She just came back to retrieve her belongings. She put out her hand and her drumstick flew into it. Then she was gone.

I had done it. I got around Gabi's wish. After all, she just said she wanted to hear Mara's Daughters. She never said she wanted to hear them *live*!

And I would keep doing it. Finding ways to make sure Gabi's wishes didn't come true. At least not the way she wanted. Until she finally agreed to give them up for good!

chapter
✦ 27 ✦

Gabi had been pretty busy while I had been out in the hall. She turned into a little wish-making machine. She now had on a brand-new outfit, straight out of the Juicy Couture catalog—a green shirred zip wrap dress and platform-heeled booties. And her hair was all loose and curled at the ends. And did I mention the makeup? She had smoky eyes, pink lips, and color on her cheeks. It looked like a professional did it. She was taking her rising star status seriously.

The cameraman was back to shooting me. Didn't this guy ever let up? "I have to go the bathroom. Don't you have to go to the bathroom, Gabi?"

"Not really," she said.

"Gabi!"

"Fine." Since Miss Simmons didn't seem to care what we were up to, we walked right out.

"No cameras in the ladies room," I declared before they followed us in.

But they started to come in, anyway! I elbowed Gabi in the side.

"She's right," Gabi said. "I wish there weren't cameras in the bathroom."

When we *finally* had some privacy, I pleaded my case one more time. "I'm begging you. Please. Undo this. Don't make me have to come up with some other way to get rid of these wishes."

She actually laughed. "You'd just cause a bigger mess. Again."

"Would not."

Gabi didn't even bother to respond. She just reached into her bag and pulled out a lip gloss and a copy of *OK!* magazine.

"Come on, Gabi. It's not funny anymore. Let's fix this. Give up the reality show, return the clothes, get Max back to normal."

"He's not so bad now."

"Maybe not to you, because he wants to be on your show. But he's still bossing everyone else around and they're just taking it. And he's not even the worst of it. There are cameras everywhere. The whole wish thing was supposed to be so I could help people, not turn them into celebutantes."

"It's helping me," she said.

I was getting the sinking feeling that Max wasn't the only monster I created with my powers.

Gabi studied her reflection in the mirror. "Elena is going to bring in Lance Gold for a photo shoot with me." Lance was Gabi's favorite actor. "She says the two of us together will help my image." Her image?! Since when did she care about that? "Can you believe it?" She sounded majorly excited. Like, well, like a girl who just found out she was going to be linked to Lance Gold.

"Pretty soon my face is going to be all over magazines like this." As she spoke her face appeared on the cover. "And not because I wished it. But because I'm such a huge celebrity. It's going to be awesome, Angel. I'm finally going to get everything I always wanted."

Gabi had a faraway look on her face.

"But that's not the way to get it."

"Why not?" She held up the magazine. "Some of these people are only famous because they have famous relatives. How different is my situation?" As she shook the magazine at me, a note dropped out.

At first I thought it was just one of those postcards

that tried to get you to order a full subscription, but it wasn't. It was another note with Gabi's name written on it from her secret admirer.

"This day just keeps getting better," she said, snagging the paper from the ground. "Do you think it's from Marc? I can't stand the suspense any longer!"

And then there it was. The signature of Gabi's secret admirer.

Cole Daniels.

My Cole Daniels.

chapter
✦ 28 ✦

She wished for Cole to like her? I didn't even
know what to say. I mean, the person I trusted more
than anyone in the whole world, the one I confided
in about my dad—the only one—basically took her
platform-heeled booties and shoved them right into
the small of my back.

"I didn't wish it," Gabi said, dropping the note on
the ground and running over to me.

"What? So he just decided he likes you better?"

"No, I don't know," she said.

I backed away from her. "You don't know!?" My
world was totally crumbling around me. "You had to
have wished it. Cole wouldn't do that. He wouldn't
send secret messages to my best friend."

"Okay, maybe I wished it, but I didn't mean it." She
wrung her hands around her neck.

Ever get stuck in a huge gust of wind where dust, leaves, and other junk were flying at you, causing your eyes to tear, and walking against it took four times your normal amount of energy? Well, that's how I felt right now. Like I was caught in a storm, only it wasn't letting up, and I had another mile to go before I could rest.

"Yeah, right," I said, my voice a hush. "Why would you wish it then? You knew what that would do to me." I backed up against the wall and slid down onto the floor. It didn't matter that it was gross and nasty. I couldn't fight the current anymore.

She started to kneel next to me, but hesitated. The floor was dirty and the garbage had overflowed to the ground. She took a deep breath and did it anyway. "Honest. I would never wish that, not on purpose."

We just sat there in silence.

"I think I know what happened," she said quietly. "When I saw you with Cole, I may have wished I had a boyfriend like him. I'm really sorry. I didn't mean for it to actually be him. I'm not like that. You know I would never steal someone's boyfriend. Especially not yours."

"Then undo it, undo everything. Take it back, Gabi," I said, trying to choke back my tears.

155

"I can't," she said, standing back up.

"You have to."

"I'll just wish for him not to like me."

I shook my head. "It doesn't work that way. You *know* that. You couldn't undo Max's attitude, and you're not going to be able to undo this. Not unless you give back all the wishes you made. It's all or nothing."

She turned away from me. "If I could just make Cole stop liking me I would. But I can't give up everything."

I stood back up. "You mean you won't."

She didn't answer.

"Gabi . . ." I could see her face in the mirror and we made eye contact through it. "If you cared about me at all, you'd undo this."

"That's not fair," she said.

"And you going out with my boyfriend is? Please."

She shook her head no. "It's not that simple."

But it was. Unless . . .

"You like him, don't you?"

"What?" she asked.

"Cole. You like him."

"No," she protested.

But I saw the look in her eyes, heard the lilt in her

voice. "You do. You like him. That's why you won't reverse this."

"That's not why."

"Liar," I shouted. "You like him, I know it. Just admit it."

"I don't," she said, but I just stared her down in the mirror until she turned to face me for real. "I mean I like him, but not . . ." Her face turned pink. "We've had Hebrew School together forever. And, yeah, I guess I've always had a little crush on him. But I always knew how much you liked him, so I never said anything. And I would NEVER go out with him. And I would never knowingly wish for him to be my boyfriend. I wouldn't do that to you."

Except that she did.

chapter

✦ 29 ✦

My boyfriend likes my best friend. MY BOYFRIEND LIKES MY BEST FRIEND. How could Gabi make this happen? How could Gabi have done this to me?

"Angel, say something," she said.

I passed out in shock when I found out my dad was the devil. But that seemed like nothing in comparison to finding out my best friend who I had known for forever was actually a boyfriend-stealing leech monster. I felt catatonic.

"Angel?"

I was so upset it was hard to talk. My fists clenched and as they did all the lightbulbs in the bathroom shorted out. It was my powers. They were going off on their own again. I needed to calm down before I accidentally did something worse, like set Gabi's hair on fire or send her to a deserted island where there were no boys for her to trick into liking her. After a few deep breaths, I managed to find my voice. "Fix this," I said in a hoarse whisper.

"I wish we had some lights that worked," she said.

Lamps appeared around the room within a fraction of a second.

"That's not what I meant." She was trying all of my patience. "Fix the Cole situation."

"You know I can't," Gabi answered. "Not without giving everything else up."

"Then give it all up."

"No," she said in a voice so low I wasn't even sure I heard her correctly.

"What?"

"I don't want to give it up."

"You mean you don't want to give *Cole* up," I seethed.

"That's not true. I like Marc. I wish he would like me."

And now with those few little words, he definitely would. She was going to have two guys dying to hang out with her, while I was miserable and alone. "Whatever, Gabi." I was fuming. "If you wanted to make things right you would. But you don't. You saw your one chance to get Cole, and you took it."

"What's that supposed to mean?" she asked, her hands on her hips. "You don't think I'm good enough for him?"

What? No way was she turning this around on me, making me the bad guy. "What it means is that he liked me, until you messed with his mind. He's not into you, Gabi, not without your hocus-pocus, so get over it."

"Right. Because someone like Cole could never like someone like me. Is that it?"

I didn't even dignify her with an answer.

"Well?" she prodded.

So I told her the truth. "Yeah, actually. He wouldn't."

"Well, you know what?" she half asked, half stated. "He was always flirting with me in Hebrew School before he started going out with you, but I ignored it. I gave up a chance with him because of you. Because I'm that good a friend."

"Oh, please," I said, my voice dripping with disgust. "Quit kidding yourself. He was never into you, and he never will be."

Her whole body stiffened. "Too bad for you," she said with a look that made the little hairs on my arms rise. "He is. And it's going to stay that way."

chapter

30

"You're going to date Cole?" I screamed. It was more than a little loud. It was an I-should-lock-the-door-so-no-one-can-come-barging-in-to-see-if-one-of-us-has-been-murdered-and-catch-it-on-camera scream.

Gabi sneered at me. "I'm not you, Angel. I'm nicer than that. I don't hurt my friends or drop them to hang out with people like Courtney."

I thought we were past that. During my brief stint as a popular girl, I hung out with Courtney and Co. even though they had a history of being really mean to Gabi. But I felt awful about it and apologized a million times since then. "So does that mean you're *not* going to go out with him?"

She didn't answer me. She just went for the door. I blocked it.

"Move, Angel."

"Answer me first," I ordered.

"NO. Move."

"Make me," I said, pressing all of my weight against the door.

"I wish you'd move."

"Ha," I said. "Your powers don't work on me."

Then she reached around me and pushed the door open. Hard. "But that does." She was strong for a toothpick with a bobble head on top. I stumbled back a few feet. Quickly grabbing onto the knob, I pulled it back shut. She went for it again.

"So that's it," I said before she could open the door, "you're going to go out and wish for whatever you want without caring who you hurt?"

"*I* know how to use my powers."

"*Your* powers? I'm the one who gave you the ability to make wishes. Anything you can do is because of me."

"Great. Because I'm going to keep using them."

"Look at yourself. You've turned into a power mutant. You need to stop before you do something stupid. Again."

"This from the expert. I wasn't the one who made a lion come out of nowhere or my shirt vanish in front of the whole school." She reached for the door again.

I used my powers to send her to the other side of the bathroom. "We're not done," I said.

"I think we are." Then a sick little smile flitted across her mouth. "I'm warning you, Angel, let me go."

"Or what?" I said.

"Or this." A second later she had a big bottle of ketchup in her hand. She squeezed it all over my shirt.

"What are you doing?" I asked, taking off the mess.

She threw a new shirt at me. It was a T-shirt with a picture of Barney on the front and the words "Fan club president" printed above. "I guess I can find a way to make my wishes work on you. Hope you like your new shirt," she said. "And from now on leave me alone or that's just the beginning. You'll regret messing with me."

And that was it. Just like that. The monster in designer couture walked out on me.

"Oh, yeah?" I shouted after her. "You're the one who's going to regret it."

She couldn't get away with that. She might have had wishes. But I had powers. This was war.

163

chapter

✦ 31 ✦

Gabi was going to pay.

As my Barney shirt and I made our way back to class, I devised the best way to get back at her.

A—use my powers.

B—try to mess up her wishes.

C—trick her into wishing for something she didn't want.

As I got closer to the classroom a sweet smell wafted by. It was a combo of roses, lilies, and a bunch of other flowers I couldn't name. When I opened the door, I found out why. The room had been converted into a botanical garden. Some little outdoor fantasy world brought inside. Gone were the science desks, microscopes, and jars of frogs. In their places were white benches, dark green grass, flowers sprouting from the floor, vines of roses covering the walls, and butterflies flying everywhere. And in the middle of it all sat Gabi. And her massage chair. Like a queen on her throne.

"Like it?" she asked when I walked in.

She was *trying* to set me off. My first reaction was to say something obnoxious, but I held back. No need to sling insults. Not when I could use "my gift" instead. But what to do? It had to be something good.

Marc handed Gabi a bouquet he plucked from the ground. "It's almost as pretty as you are."

"Ha!" I said loud enough for everyone to hear. I mean, come on, it was a lame line. And he didn't even mean it. He only said it because Gabi wished for him to like her.

"Oh, you think that's funny?" she asked, glaring at me. "You don't think anyone could find me pretty? Well, he's not the only one who does. I *wish* Cole would tell me how much he likes me."

That girl was evil. If I didn't know better, I'd guess she was one of those demons Mara's Daughters said lived on earth.

My whole body stiffened as Cole pushed through a rosebush, cameras, and about six other people to get to Gabi. "Did you get my note?" he asked, picking at some petals. "I've wanted to tell you about it before, but, I don't know, I just didn't. Everything I wrote is true, though."

"Cole," I shrieked. What he had written was that he thought she was beautiful and amazing! That he wanted to date her!

"Sorry, Angel." He gave me a half smile and a little shrug. "I just don't feel that way about you anymore. I like Gabi better."

It's because of the wish. It's because of the wish. It's because of the wish. I kept telling myself that, and yet it didn't make me feel any better. Cole didn't even care that he was pulverizing my heart. He only cared about Gabi. The worst best friend ever.

"Would you go out with me?" he asked her. "I've always thought you were really pretty and sweet."

Always? Always! No. No. NO. NO. This wasn't happening. I moved to the back of the room. I couldn't watch anymore. This was awful. Worse than that. But I didn't have the words, because there weren't any to describe what it felt like to see the guy of your dreams and your best friend use your heart like a hacky sack.

It just royally stunk.

And I was going to make it stink a little more with the help of my powers. Let's see how lovey-dovey Cole felt when he was stuck in a room that smelled like skunk. It was time to destroy Gabi's little love paradise.

I closed my eyes and thought about an awful smell filling the room. Armpits mixed with cottage cheese left out for a week, and some pickle juice thrown in. Something to totally overpower the roses and lilies and love in the room.

My eyes teared up. And not just because of the Cole/Gabi situation. But because the smell was putrid. It stung the air. It was working.

"What is that?" I heard one person yell out. "Where's it coming from?" another said. When I opened my eyes, I saw a few people sniffing around, trying to locate the source. Ha! Maybe Cole would think about the odor every time he thought about asking Gabi out.

"Uck," Max said, his nose near my head. "It's Angel."

He was such a jerk. "No, it's not. It's the whole room."

"No, it's definitely you." He stepped back while covering his nose with one hand.

I lowered my face to my shoulder and took a whiff. Gross. It was me! I messed up. Big surprise. Why couldn't anything ever go my way?

"As president of the Barney fan club," he said, pointing to my shirt with his free hand, "are you in charge of cleaning up after him? Did you bring the pooper-scooper to class with you?"

First of all, Barney was not a dog. He didn't poop in the park. And second. OMG. I reeked. Bad.

"Cut it out, Max," Courtney said, coming up to me. "It's all right, Angel. A lot of people suffer from BO, but it's okay. Maybe you just need a stronger deodorant. I have some in my gym locker if you want to use it."

"I do not have body odor," I shouted, hoping to activate my powers. It wasn't working. "This is a science class." At least it used to be. "All sorts of smelly things are stored here. Something just exploded."

"Yeah, onto you," Max said.

"I can't take the rotten-egg smell," Elena said. "Let's move to another room. Angel, you can stay here."

"The odor is going away," I said. As I spoke, I concentrated on the smell disappearing. Finally it did. But the teasing remained.

"Thank God," Max said. "But maybe instead of Double-A we should call her BO."

"Leave her alone," Courtney told him.

Lana and Jaydin backed her up, nodding like crazy.

Gabi walked over and whispered in my ear. "Nice. I guess it doesn't matter that my wishes don't work on you. You take care of your own payback. So stop trying to mess with me."

Me with her!? Try the other way around. I wasn't the boy-stealing, wish-crazy egomaniac. She was!

My world had shifted a hundred and eighty degrees.

Courtney and Co. were the ones coming to my rescue while Gabi was the one trying to destroy me.

This was not over.

chapter

✦ 32 ✦

Gabi needed to be stopped. She wished to be a star. Well, I was going to make sure she got the full star treatment.

"Elena," I said, flashing my dimples. "I'm sorry I've been so difficult. I really do want to help Gabi be a star."

"Good," she said.

"Just tell me what I need to do. Oh," I added, putting my plan into motion, "how important is it for stars to stay in shape? Should I get Gabi to the gym?"

"You know, exercise *is* very important." I could see her wheels turning. "Gabi, let's get you to do a few laps around the track, some sit-ups, crunches, yoga."

Ha! Gabi hated to exercise. About as much as I hated math. Which was a lot.

"No," she protested.

"It's part of being a star," Elena said.

"Since when?" she asked.

Since I put it in Elena's head.

"You could always just give up what you have. *Give it all up,*" I said. "Then you wouldn't have to spend hours working out."

The corners of Gabi's mouth slowly turned upward until she had a big grin on her face. I knew her well enough. She was up to something. Something big. "Elena," she said, "don't some stars get their exercise from dancing?"

Elena nodded.

"Great," Gabi said. "I wish I could do it that way."

Hip-hop music started pumping through the intercom in the class. "Works for me," Elena said.

"You can't beat me," she whispered to me. "Hey, Cole," Gabi said. "Want to dance?" She made sure to send me a big, old smirk.

"Absolutely," he said.

Once they started, the whole class turned into a dance party. Everyone was shaking their hips and moving their bodies to the music. At least it was a fast song. Still, I didn't like Cole anywhere near Gabi.

"Marc," I said, nudging him. "How can you let some other guy dance with Gabi? Go cut in."

"I don't know," he said, shrugging his shoulder. "She asked Cole. Not me."

"Trust me." I gave him a push in her direction. "I'm her best friend. She likes *you*. She's only trying to make you jealous. Now go."

"Really?"

"Yes!" I practically pushed him three feet toward Gabi. "Dance already."

He did. And he even managed to wedge his way between Cole and Gabi. My work was done. Until Gabi opened her mouth again.

"Cole, don't go away. I can dance with you both."

With them *both*? Who did Gabi think she was? I wasn't letting her have two guys. Especially when one of them was mine.

With a wave of my hand, I sent Gabi flying backward. At least that was one power I knew how to control. "Oops, what happened, Gabi?" I acted all innocent.

"Nothing," she said, doing some stupid move back to Cole and Marc where she pretended to throw out a fishing line and reel them in.

I sent her backward again. Nobody even thought anything about it. They probably figured she was just making the most of the space—showing off on the dance floor.

"Amateur hour," she said to me, and gestured for the guys to come closer. "I wish it was a slow song. Cole, I'll dance with you first." The music changed, and Cole reached out to put his arms around Gabi.

"No!" I sent her flying again. Or I tried to. But I wasn't fast enough. Cole already had his arm around her and instead of sending her away, I sent them both tumbling to the ground.

He fell right on her!

"Sorry," Cole said, standing up. His cheeks were all pink, and he put out his hand to help her up.

She took it. And he actually interlocked their fingers and gave her one of those cute, lopsided grins of his that always made me all melty. I hadn't meant for that to happen. I wanted to keep them apart, not push them closer together.

"I'll help her," I said, cutting in, trying to nudge my way between them. They needed to be separated.

"That's okay," Cole said, not taking his eyes off Gabi. "I like helping her. I like everything about her."

It didn't matter to him what I thought, how I felt. All that mattered was Gabi. I couldn't take it anymore.

chapter
✦ 33 ✦

"Where are you going?" The cameraman chased after me as I booked down the hall.

"Bathroom, now leave me alone."

"You just went to the bathroom."

Why did this guy care how often I had to pee? "Maybe I have a small bladder, okay?" They were *so* going to air that on the reality show. I was going to be the smelly girl who had to use the toilet every three minutes.

But who cared? Nothing mattered anymore. I lost my dad, my best friend, and my boyfriend all in one week. And to top it off, my attempts to do good in the world were all failing.

When I finally got inside the bathroom, I sat down with my back up against the door. I thought the silence and getting away from everyone would be comforting, help me relax. But it was the opposite. I just kept picturing Cole reaching out for Gabi's hand. It was like one of those sappy perfume commercials where the guy helps the woman up from a puddle and then they go on to live happily ever after. While me, I was probably doomed to shoveling coal in the underworld. And then I'd be depressed forever. Shoveling *coal* would just remind me of *Cole*. My Cole. The Cole that ditched me for Gabi.

How could I get him to notice me? I crossed my arms around my chest. My nonexistent one. And then it occurred to me. Maybe if I had boobs Cole would look at me. They'd give me an edge over Gabi. She didn't have any, either.

But it wasn't like they were going to grow overnight—if ever. Unless . . .

No. I couldn't. Could I?

I looked down at my shirt. Yeah, my powers had messed up before. But this was worth the risk. Instead of Double-A, I could be Double-D. That was pretty good motivation. And since the bathroom was quiet, I could focus, really concentrate on making them grow. Lou always said concentration and powers went hand in hand. Although, he'd probably flip out if he knew what I had in mind. Even more incentive!

Big boobs here I come. I was going for it.

I slapped my hands over my chest and closed my eyes and chanted, "Grow, grow, grow, grow, grow."

Nothing was happening. I was still flat as an ironing board. "Come on," I groaned. Why wasn't this working? I even made up a rhyme. "Come on chest, be the best, be bigger than all the rest."

Still nothing.

I needed to clear my mind. No Gabi, no Cole. Just my boobs getting bigger. I envisioned it, saw myself actually needing a bra—not just wearing one to wear one—and all of a sudden, my hands pushed outward. My boobs were growing.

Yes!

And growing.

Uhhh.

And growing!!!

OMG!!!

They wouldn't stop. They were getting massive. Like all of my teachers' boobs combined. And then some. *Please stop! Please stop! Please stop! Please stop!*

Finally, after what seemed like two and a half lifetimes, they did. I looked in the mirror and let out a slight gasp. My powers worked all right. Too well.

My shirt was completely stretched to the limit. Barney looked like he'd gained two hundred pounds, his face was so stretched. And the boobs hiked my shirt up putting my belly on display for the world to see. How was I going to explain this?

This wasn't what I had in mind. I *had* wanted big boobs. But not bowling balls.

"Go back to your normal size," I said. I tried pushing them, hoping they'd flatten back down, but they wouldn't. This was bad. I kept trying. Then I heard a couple of voices nearing the bathroom. No one could see me like this. I needed to hide in one of the stalls. But I hadn't moved quickly enough. The door to the bathroom was opening.

I used my powers to hold it shut. "All full in here. Use the one down the hall," I said.

But the person on the other side wasn't giving up.

"Come on. Open up. I just want to use the mirror."

"Busy," I answered.

"What are you doing? I'm getting a teacher," the voice on the other side said.

I didn't need to draw more attention to myself. I had to make a break for it. So I opened the door and bolted.

chapter
✦ 34 ✦

I was definitely getting in my exercise for the day. The cameraman, too. He was right behind me as I made my way through the halls. Running with boobs was weird. They felt like two bean bags strapped to my chest. I held up my arms to cover them, to keep them still. But there was no stopping. Not with the cameraman on my tail.

He couldn't film me with these things. I could just imagine what people would think when they saw them. That I balled up toilet paper—seven rolls worth—in my bra, or put balloons or melons in there. It was disastrous. Being Double-A was bad, but being a bra stuffer was even worse. People would be flinging dirty tissues at me for the rest of my existence.

We neared the corner. I was about twenty feet ahead of him. It was my only shot. I had to duck into a room before he made the turn and saw where I went. The second one on the right looked empty. I made my move.

I held my breath and waited, but no one followed me in. I took a look around. There was a couch, a coffee machine, a TV. The teachers' lounge—where they went to get away from all of us. I had never been inside before. It was pretty cool.

The closet drew my attention. There had to be something in there to cover up my chest. The selection wasn't big. I saw a man's suit jacket, a fleece hoodie, and a trench coat. I grabbed the trench coat. It was way too old-looking for me, but I didn't care. It would do the trick.

I put it on, closed the belt, and shoved my hands in the pockets. There was a pair of sunglasses inside. I threw them on, too. Anything to help keep that cameraman from recognizing me.

Just then the door to the lounge creaked open. As casually as I could, I moved to the coffee machine, keeping my back to the door. Whoever it was just needed to think I was a teacher.

"Can I help you?"

It was the principal, Mr. Stanton. His low, no-nonsense voice couldn't be mistaken.

I shook my head no.

"What are you doing in here, Miss Garrett?"

How'd he know it was me? I didn't even say anything. Guess I was the only person in Goode Middle School with fire-engine-red hair. I took off the sunglasses and gave him a tiny smile. He didn't look amused. "I'm going to repeat myself," he said. "What are you doing in here?"

There was no way I was getting in trouble. I needed an excuse. Something he'd go for. "Max!" I said. "Max wanted a cup of coffee and asked me to come in here and get it for him."

"Oh," Mr. Stanton said. "Why didn't you say so? He's a fine young man. What that boy wants he should get." Stanton was under the Max spell like almost everyone else.

And since helping Max got me in this mess, it was only fitting that I used him to get me out of it—at least part of it. "Exactly."

The bell sounded, and I grabbed a cup of coffee. "I'd better go."

I needed to make my escape while the halls were busy. It was easier to get lost in a crowd. And I needed to get to Gabi—without being followed. It was time to put an end to this giant mess.

chapter

35

I rushed to my locker with my head down. Gabi's was a few feet away from mine, and she tended to stop there after science class. The plan was to grab her, lock us in a classroom, and keep her trapped until she agreed to undo the wishes. That's right, I was going to star-nap her. It was my only choice. My powers weren't working, and I needed an alternative.

I glanced up. She was there all right. And Cole was with her!

They were laughing about something. Probably me. And that was without even seeing my new boobs. I took a step closer. "So can we grab that movie on Friday?" he asked her.

Say no, Gabi.

"I already told you," she said, dropping her head slightly. A piece of hair fell in front of her face. Cole pushed it away and his hand just stayed there on her cheek. And he wouldn't stop looking at her. Then he leaned in.

HE WAS GOING TO KISS HER!

I was holding one of those old-school Styrofoam cups of coffee in my hand and without even realizing it, I crushed it, sending hot liquid all over myself. I let out a shriek of pain. Everyone turned to look at me.

"Angel," Gabi said. "It's not what it looks like."

"Don't bother." I didn't need to hear her phony explanations. She already made Cole like her, told the whole class about it, and danced with him in front of me. A kiss was the obvious next step. Why would I give her the benefit of the doubt?

My whole body was shaking. I needed to calm down before my powers went off on their own. But I couldn't get my heartbeat under control. It was on turbo speed. Not even deep breaths were helping. Each one just made it worse. *Relax,* I thought as I exhaled. *Relax . . . Relax . . .* But I couldn't calm down. A nightmare was coming to life in front of my very eyes. I hated Gabi. It didn't matter that we were best friends. She was destroying me. I didn't owe her anything.

Only revenge.

Suddenly, an awful smell filled the air. Like a tuna fish sandwich someone left in the back of a car for a week.

"Double-A, you did it again. Control yourself!" Max said, waving his hand in front of his face.

Oh no. Did I accidentally turn myself into a stink bomb again? Was it the big boobs? Had I accidentally filled them with toxic waste? I took a whiff. It wasn't me. What was going on? What did I do?

Then I saw it turn the corner. A mutant guy with hollow, sunken eyes, ripped clothes, sagging skin, and a wide-open mouth, showing off his razor-sharp teeth. It was a zombie. . . .

My *nightmare* coming to life.

chapter
✦ 36 ✦

If I didn't do something quick, everyone was going to be zombie food. Why did I have to think of a *nightmare*? I guess it was fresh in my mind from the one I had the night before. A zombie chased me down, wanting me to grant his wish. Which was having me for lunch. But at least in the dream no one else was around. Here, the creature could have a feeding fest. And it would be all my fault. I really was a bad luck charm.

A few people shouted "What is that?" and "It's coming right for us."

I concentrated on making the monster disappear. But just like my boobs—it wouldn't go away. And I didn't have much more time. It was fast approaching.

"Gabi," I shrieked, "wish the zombie away."

"It's not working. I've been trying," she yelled back.

She couldn't undo my powers, either. "Then wish that no one was in the hallway right now, except me and that *thing*. DO IT. NOW!"

For once today, she didn't argue. In a flash everyone was gone. It was just me and the zombie. Face to face. I wasn't a fool. I ran. All those horror movies that make you think zombies are slow and can't move are wrong. This one was fast. Maybe because I dreamed him that way.

What did I know about zombies? Obviously they were fast. But they were also supposed to be dumb. It was time to find out. *Please let me have created a stupid zombie.*

Instead of trapping Gabi, I needed to trap the monster. I opened the door to an empty classroom. "Angel's in there!" I said, pointing wildly inside.

It worked. The zombie went inside looking for Angel. I slammed the door shut, locking him inside, away from me and everyone. Yes! I did it! Finally something good. The hallways were safe again. Or so I thought.

"Angel?"

"Lou!" What was he doing here? I steered him away

from the zombie classroom. I didn't want him looking in and seeing what I'd been up to. I was putting a whole school in harm's way with my monster. Even Lou wouldn't do that.

"You need to go."

"Are you all right? You seem nervous and out of breath."

"Well. Yeah, um, wouldn't you be nervous? Talking to the devil himself?"

He raised an eyebrow at me. "What's really going on?"

"Nothing. I just want you gone."

The zombie let out a roar and banged on the door. "Drama class," I said. "They scream a lot. Gets out tension, lets them find their inner voice or something. Now will you please go? I don't want anyone in school to see you."

"Angel . . ."

"I mean it. Go."

He shook his head at me. "Fine, but we're going to talk later. I need to tell you something."

"Yeah, whatever," I said, bracing myself against a locker. "Just get out of here."

Lou studied me for a minute and his face sort of fell. He looked hurt. Then he just disappeared.

I let out a breath. One problem down. But then I noticed something out of the corner of my eye. The cameraman who had been following me earlier was inside the classroom across the hall. He had his camera up to the window in the door. And he was filming!

Everything that just happened was caught on tape.

chapter
✦ 37 ✦

Lou disappearing. A zombie chasing me. My giant boobs. And it was all on-camera.

I needed to get it. I waved at the cameraman and walked toward him. He was going to fork over the film or I'd steal it. One way or another it was going to be mine.

When I got up to the door, he wouldn't open it. But he did keep shooting.

"Let me in!"

He shook his head no frantically and pointed like a madman with his free hand.

"I just want the tape." I turned the knob, but it wouldn't budge. "Come on."

"Run," he yelled.

"Huh?"

The sound of snapping teeth made me turn around.

The zombie had gotten out and was headed straight for me. With a flick of my arm I sent him sailing down the hallway. Then I took the camera guy's advice and ran.

What was I going to do? The list of problems I'd created kept growing.

I couldn't ask Lou for help. Maybe Mara's Daughters? They had powers, too. And they claimed to be the good kind of demons. But what if they weren't? What if everyone from the underworld eventually succumbed to evil? Even me. No. I got myself into this mess. I was going to fix it.

The footsteps behind me were getting louder. I turned my head. The zombie was gaining on me, and he looked really ticked. He let out a humongous roar. I screamed, too. I was living a horror movie. Hopefully I was the lead—not some sidekick. The leads never died. I sent the creature flying again. But while that happened, I wasn't really watching where I was going, and I ran right into the water fountain, then fell backward onto my butt. This wasn't the time to be clumsy. This was the time to find an escape. But I couldn't.

The monster was coming toward me again. How many times could I keep sending him away before he actually caught me—or gave up and went for one of my classmates?

It was hopeless.

Then it got worse.

An arm appeared from the janitor's closet and pulled me inside.

I did the only sensible thing.

I screamed.

chapter 38

This was it. I fell right into a trap. I must have created two zombies. The up side was that my problems were finally going to be over—I would no longer be alive to see them. I was going to be Angel food. Not the fluffy white cake kind. But the dark meat made *from* me kind.

"Shh," it said in a harsh whisper. "Promise not to scream, and I'll let you go."

This zombie spoke perfect English. "Promise?" it asked.

The thing had me gripped from behind, so I didn't even know what it looked like. How could I promise not to scream? What if its eyeballs were hanging out? That was definitely scream-worthy. But I decided to take my chances. I shook my head yes, and it let go.

I turned to face the creature. Only it wasn't a creature. It was just D.L.

Maybe I should have stuck with running from the zombie. D.L. probably wanted to use me as bait, offer me up to the monster on a plate, in exchange for letting him go free.

I pinned myself against the door. "What do you want with me?"

"Please," D.L. said. "Don't flatter yourself. What would I want from you?"

Okay, maybe he didn't want to feed me to a monster, but he was still a jerk.

"And you're welcome," he said.

Well, maybe not that big a jerk. He did just hide me from the zombie. "Thanks," I said, and slid down to the ground.

"What are you doing in here, anyway?" I asked, making sure my coat was still closed. I didn't need him seeing my new chest.

"It was the only place to get away from those cameras. There's like five different cameramen roaming around trying to get set-up shots for that show and interviews about Gabi. And I don't know what they're doing now. It's like they're trying to turn it into a haunted house."

Ooh! He thought the zombie was part of the show. Hopefully everyone else would, too! "And you don't want to be on TV?" I asked. "I would think someone like you would love it."

"Someone like me?" His lip curled and he flung his head back, moving his hair from in front of his eye. "What does that mean?"

Umm. What it meant was someone hot and completely self-centered. But I wasn't going to tell him that—well, the hot part, anyway. "You just seem the type."

"Well, you don't know me."

I knew that he was a complete snob. The first time I met him, he wouldn't talk to me because he was afraid I'd hurt his "cool" reputation. I knew he loved to make fun of me and get people into trouble. And I knew he was into girls like Courtney Lourde—the mean Courtney Lourde—so I knew more than enough.

"You could have just gone home," I said.

"Tried. Got busted."

I didn't really know what to say next. It wasn't like D.L. and I were friends. More like the opposite. So we just sat there not speaking. But I could feel him looking at me. I glanced down when I felt a warm blush filling my cheeks. It wasn't like I was into him or anything. I mean, he was D.L. Helper after all. But his eyes were this aqua blue. They were kind of mesmerizing.

"Why'd you help me?" I asked to break the silence.

D.L. shrugged. "All that screaming, it sounded like you needed it."

I was so surprised he bothered to help. I would have expected him to push me right toward the thing. "Thanks. I kind of got myself in over my head."

He didn't respond, so I kept talking. It was better than just sitting there looking into his eyes. "The zombie won't stop chasing me. I need to figure out a way to convince the, umm, producers to get rid of it. All that and Gabi and I are in a war. Overall, my life is falling apart."

It actually felt good to talk to someone. Even if that someone was D.L.

"So fix it," he said.

"Thanks. Like I haven't been trying?"

He whipped back his hair again. "I think if you wanted to put an end to this madness, you would have. Just do it."

"You don't understand the nightmare I'm living." That was the truth.

He shrugged his shoulder. "Nightmares don't last forever."

I thought about this for a moment. It's true—nightmares *don't* last forever. Was it possible that if I played out the entire dream from last night it would eventually end? That the zombie would dematerialize? It was a risk. Because in the nightmare the zombie actually caught me right before I woke up. If I was wrong, I was lunchmeat. But if I was right, the nightmare would be over. The zombie would disappear right after it caught me.

That would take care of one problem, but I still had Gabi to deal with. I bit my nail and tried to come up with a plan. What was I supposed to do? I felt D.L. staring at me. Oh no. Did he notice my mongo boobs? I peeked up at him. Luckily it was my face he was studying.

It was weird having him look at me without slinging insults my direction. "I'm just trying to come up with a way to make Gabi give up her . . . um . . . her . . ." I almost said wishes. That would have gone over beautifully.

"Reality show," he offered.

"Yeah," I said, relieved to have a sensible answer—one I should have been able to come up with in a heartbeat. Why was my brain getting all soupy around him? I was probably just in shock that he wasn't acting like his usual mean self. Maybe Gabi wished he'd turn nice like Courtney and Co.

"Those shows make fools out of people. Just make her realize it."

He was onto something.

I knew just what to do. It was time for Gabi to play the fool.

chapter

39

It was hard to believe these words were coming out of my mouth, but I turned to D.L. and said, "Any chance you want to help me?"

He just looked at me.

"I think I know how we can get the cameras out of school and maybe put life back to normal."

"Fine," he said. "What do you want me to do?"

"Help set Operation Shut Down Gabi into motion." I just needed D.L. to make sure Goode's new little star and her fans went to the auditorium, while I dealt with my other nightmare. "It shouldn't be too hard," I told him after I explained what I needed. "Just tell them Lance Gold is in there. Gabi told me Elena was setting up a photo shoot with him, so everyone should buy it."

He agreed.

"Okay," I said, cracking the door open. "Ready or not. Oh . . ." I turned back to him. "If anyone gives you a hard time, just tell them it's what Max wants. They'll listen."

D.L. rolled his eyes. "Let's just do this."

I took one more second to think about the fact that D.L. was actually helping me, then shoved my head out the door. The zombie was down the hall to my left baring his teeth and smashing lockers as he passed them. He was angry. He was *hungry*. "Go *that* way." I pointed D.L. to the right. I needed him to round up everyone. The zombie was *my* problem. And once I got rid of it, I'd put a stop to that other monster. Gabi.

D.L. and I parted ways.

After he was out of sight, I called out to the zombie. "Yo, Night of the Living Dead, over here."

Please don't let this be a big mistake! I thought as the creature made its way toward me. If my thinking was correct, the zombie would disappear. If I was wrong, well, I didn't want to think about that.

It was a gamble. A big one. But I was going to see my nightmare through.

A second later the zombie was in front of me. It reached its arm out. It was big and muscular, with nails that looked like they could rip through flesh. Survival instinct kicked in. I couldn't help it. I waved my hand, sending the zombie backward. It let out a roar.

"Attention, everyone," a voice—D.L.'s—came over the loud speaker. "Everyone to the auditorium now."

Mr. Stanton could be heard in the background. "Put the microphone down, young man."

"Max sent me," D.L. mumbled. Mr. Stanton didn't seem to answer. "Lance Gold is in there, everyone. We need you to go to the auditorium now."

D.L. did his part, but was I brave enough to do mine?

"Go now," D.L. repeated. "Do it for Max."

Those words played over and over in my head as the zombie headed back in my direction. *Do it for Max. Do it for Max.* If I got rid of the zombie, I could work on fixing everything else. Turning Max back into his old self again, getting rid of the reality show, taking Cole out from under Gabi's spell, my boobs.

I *was* going to do it for Max. And I was going to do it for *me*. It was time to face up to all the trouble I'd caused. And with that, I stepped forward and let the zombie grab me.

chapter

The zombie's hands circled around my arms. Why wasn't it disappearing? Was my theory about letting the nightmare run its course wrong? My body actually started to tremble. The thing opened its mouth, showing off its teeth. Last night I woke up right as it, he, whatever it was, was about to take a chunk out of my bicep.

But that's not what seemed to be happening.

The monster was still big as life, and it was going in for the kill.

"Noooo!" I screamed, closing my eyes and bracing for the pain of razor-sharp teeth cutting into me.

Only it never happened. I opened one eye, then the other. The zombie was gone! How could I almost have forgotten the scream?! It's what woke me up from my dream the other night. My plan worked. I saw the nightmare out to the end, and I was still in one piece! I took a few deep breaths. The shaking finally stopped. I was okay. Now it was time to make my other plan work.

Operation Shut Down Gabi.

The auditorium was packed when I walked in, and it was pretty noisy. There were a lot of people asking about Lance. And others still freaked out about the monster they had seen earlier walking the halls.

I jumped up onstage. "Excuse me, everyone." But no one paid any attention. Except the cameras. It took me a while to get everyone to be quiet. Eventually I just said I was Gabi's BFF, and they finally listened.

"Hi," I said. "I know you're all waiting for Lance. But first, I have a couple of things to tell you. That zombie you saw in the hall. Um, he's an actor. He heard there was a reality show filming here and was hoping to get on TV. He apologizes if he scared anyone." I hoped they were buying it. "Second, I'd like to call Gabi Gottlieb up here. Come on, Gabi. A star should be center stage. Everyone give her a round of applause as she makes her way up."

People clapped like crazy. Gabi didn't have much choice. She came up onstage, but she didn't look happy about it. She smiled at the crowd, but spoke to me through gritted teeth. "What are you up to?"

She was going to have to wait and see, just like everyone else.

"As many of you know," I said into the microphone, "Gabi is my best friend. So I thought I'd share a few of my favorite stories about her with you. Like the time she peed her pants in school while she was sitting at her desk. The teacher sent everyone to the library as a cover up. But it was really so no one would point at Gabi and make fun of her."

"That was in kindergarten," Gabi screamed.

"But don't you *wish* it was now?" Okay, I didn't think that would work—that she'd actually go to the bathroom in front of everyone. But the story annoyed her, and that's what I was going for. At least for the moment.

"No!" she screamed.

If I wanted to make her accidentally wish for something, it was going to have to be something she actually wanted. It was up to me to paint the scene.

"Another thing about Gabi is . . ."

"Enough, Angel," she said. "I wish you'd stop."

But her wishes didn't work on me.

I continued, "She loves junk food. If she could, she'd dive into a giant bowl of ice cream, with fudge, whipped cream, sprinkles, the works. Who wouldn't want a huge tub of ice cream to feast on? All that chocolatey goodness. Doesn't that sound amazing? Don't you wish you had that right now, Gabi?"

"No," she said, but I knew she was thinking about it.

"Are you sure? All the ice cream you could eat right there in front of you. Heaps of whipped cream. All the fudge you could want, and the pick of any flavor of ice cream. Mint chocolate chip. Chubby Hubby. Triple chocolate chunk with Oreo bits? Don't you just want to take a huge bite?"

A second later Gabi was standing over a massive bowl of ice cream, scooping a handful of fudge into her mouth. The bowl was about the size of one of the spinning teacups in Disney World. I knew it would work! Make her visualize it and there it was.

It was almost like someone had hypnotized her. When she realized what she was doing, she dropped her hands from her mouth. But chocolate was already dribbling down her chin.

People in the audience laughed.

It wasn't every day you saw a girl eating a giant ice cream sundae with her hands.

My plan was working; if I could make Gabi think

about something she liked, she'd wish for it—even if it wasn't the right time or place.

"Embarrassing, huh, Gabi? You have to be careful what you wish for. I know you like ice cream, but a vat of it?"

"Whatever," Gabi said. "It doesn't matter."

But her eyes told another story. She was definitely embarrassed.

Angel–1.

Gabi–0.

Then I went for phase two of the plan. "I'm sorry. It's my fault," I said, pretending to actually care. "I shouldn't have put that image in your head. But you can always just wish you were in your warm, nice bed, under the covers. It would have to beat this."

Just like I knew she would, Gabi wished to be in her bed. And lo and behold, there she was in her bed, in the middle of the stage, in front of the entire school. The same bed where she kept her huge stuffed animal collection.

"Oh," I said, walking over and picking up an alligator in a pink frilly dress, "did I mention that Gabi plays with stuffed animals? This one she named Alli and she gives it this squeaky little voice. Do it for us, Gabi."

She glared at me. Ha! It was only a matter of time before she would cave. If she didn't, I'd never let up on her. And she knew it. I totally won this war.

"No? How about this one?" I picked up a lion. "She named it Rori after her sister. Real cool, huh?" I shook the lion in front of her face. "Hi, Gabi, did you miss me?" I asked in my best Rori the lion voice. There was more laughter.

Gabi's hands clenched into fists. "You're not getting away with this," she said. "I wish everyone thought playing with stuffed animals was incredibly cool."

"Awww," someone yelled out from the audience. "Can I play with them?"

"Me too," another said.

"Well, look at that." Gabi gave me a smile. A big phony one. "I beat you at your own game. Want to give up now? Or do you want me to show you how I'm going to keep winning?"

Boy, was she asking for it. She was so going to regret messing with—

Oh my gosh.

What was I saying? Was I turning into my father?

Revenge? Humiliation? Wasn't that something the devil would do?

I didn't want to be Lou. Yet my actions seemed to

be coming straight from some underworld handbook.

This whole mess started because I wanted to do something good. And yet now I was trying to strike out against a girl who I referred to as my best friend this morning. Yes, Gabi majorly hurt me. But did I need to hurt her back? Not if I didn't want to follow in my dad's footsteps.

There had to be another way to fix the messes I caused. Another way to convince Gabi to give up the wishes.

And I was pretty sure I'd figured out how.

chapter

41

I was taking a big gamble with our friendship. It was either the most brilliant idea I've ever had or the most stupid one. It was hard to tell. I wouldn't know for sure until after the fact—and then it would be too late. But first I had to trick Gabi into making one more wish.

"Not letting up," I told her through gritted teeth as I waved to the audience. "I'm going to keep bugging and bugging and bugging you."

"Just try it," she said.

"Fine. How about I share another story. Maybe the time *someone* farted in French class," I said, my voice once again getting louder so the whole auditorium could hear, "and it smelled so bad but no one knew—"

"Shut up, Angel."

"What? Do you wish I'd stop? You know your

wishes about me don't work." I could tell how frustrated Gabi was feeling by the way her jaw throbbed. "But maybe," I started with a taunting tone, "you wish that as far as the *rest* of the world was concerned I didn't exist?"

"Yeah," she said. "I do."

Gabi got her wish.

Just like that, I no longer existed. Not to anyone but Gabi. And I guess to Lou, too. To the rest of the world it was like Angel Garrett was never born. And the only two people who knew better, who I could actually communicate with, were the two I wasn't exactly on great speaking terms with.

"Well, I guess you're happy now," I told her.

"What are you talking about?"

"*Everyone* thinks I don't exist. Thanks to your wish," I informed her.

She rolled her eyes. "Yeah, right."

To prove my point I yelled out to the crowd that Lance Gold was here and to give a round of applause. Not one person acknowledged me.

"That doesn't mean anything," Gabi said. "They just don't believe you."

"Watch this." I belted out *Somewhere Over the Rainbow*. And my a cappella singing is not to be ignored. Not unless you're under a spell. It's plug your ears, tell me to be quiet, stuff an apple in my mouth bad. *American Idol* reject–worthy. And no one so much as covered their ears.

Gabi's eyes got wide. "I just wanted you to stop bothering me."

"You got a lot more than that." I sat down on the stage.

"Well," she said, giving me a weak smile. "This will give you the perfect reason to transfer to a new school. Maybe you'll even be popular there."

Transfer! That was her solution? Not "let me fix this, I'd never let you stay this way?" "How will I do that?" I shrieked. "No one knows I exist!"

"Only people here are affected by the wish. Like what happened with Max."

"It's not the same." My voice was getting even louder. "The wording wasn't *in* school. It was *to the rest of the world*. My life is over."

Gabi paced back and forth. "This is ridiculous. It can't be everyone. Call your mom."

"There's no point."

"Just do it," she ordered.

I dialed my mother and put her on speaker. "Mom?" I said.

But my mother acted like there wasn't anyone on the other end of the phone. "Who is this, please? Is anyone there? Please speak up."

"Mom, it's me. Angel."

"Hello?" Mom said.

I knew the wish included her. I knew she'd act like I didn't exist, yet actually experiencing it was eerie. This was my mother! The woman who claimed to see auras! How could she not sense her very own daughter?

My skin started to prickle. What if I bet wrong? What if Gabi wouldn't give up her wishes? Then what? Would I have to go the rest of my life without speaking to the world? To my mom? Sure, I sometimes wished for that—that she'd leave me alone—forever. But I didn't really mean it.

Now the closest I'd ever get to communicating with her was moving the wand on her Ouija board, pretending to be some spirit.

"Mrs. Garrett," Gabi said.

"Oh, Gabi, it's you," my mom said. "Aren't you the talk of the town!"

"I guess," she said. "But Mrs. Garrett, I actually have Angel here. Don't you want to talk to her?"

"To who?"

"Your *daughter*."

My mom laughed. LAUGHED. "I don't have a daughter."

The words grabbed hold of my spinal cord and squeezed. *I don't have a daughter.*

I clicked the phone off. I couldn't listen to another word. This was getting too real. "See!" Before it was a game, a plan to get Gabi to give up the wishes. But it didn't feel like a game anymore. I looked up at Gabi, but she wouldn't look back at me. I knew what that meant—I bet wrong. Gabi was picking the wishes. Not me.

"I wish people wouldn't ignore you," she said.

But that wasn't enough to fix it. "That doesn't help. You know you can't just undo one wish. It's all or nothing.

"I'm sorry," she said.

"Who are you talking to?" Max called out.

"No one," Gabi shot back.

And she was right. Because from here on out, I really was no one.

I'd gambled and lost.

chapter

✦ 42 ✦

Everyone in the auditorium was talking to one
another. Laughing. Waiting for Lance. Not me. Tears
welled up in my eyes. My very own best friend—former
best friend—was going to let me walk the earth like
a zombie. Only I wouldn't eat people. I would just
wander around unable to communicate with anyone.
I'd be the living dead. "I can't believe you're leaving
me like this."

"You idiot," she said.

Now she was calling me names. But it was accurate.
Thinking that she'd put our friendship first *was* idiotic.
She stole Cole. There wasn't anything she wouldn't
do. Even sacrifice me for the sake of her wishes.

"Of course I wouldn't leave you like this."

What did she say? "Can you repeat that?"

She crossed her arms in front of her and looked

down at me. "Do you really think I'd let you go through the rest of your life like a freaky mutant?" She smiled a little. "More than you already are?"

I shrugged my shoulder. The truth was, yes, I did.

She sat down next to me. "I wouldn't do that."

"You took Cole."

Gabi bit her lip. "That was an accident."

"It wasn't an accident when you made him announce his feelings about you or dance in the middle of science class . . . or when you kissed him!"

"I didn't kiss him," she protested.

"Only because I walked in on you."

"No. Because I wouldn't do that."

"Then why'd do you do all that other stuff with him?" I focused on my fingernails, which were gnawed down to practically nothing.

"I was mad at you."

"Mad at *me*?" I moved my focus to Gabi. "You're the one who wished for my boyfriend to like you."

"I told you that wasn't on purpose. I just wished someone like him would like me. I didn't mean for it to really happen. But when I tried to explain it to you, you started saying all these things that made it sound like I wasn't good enough for Cole." She looked up. It seemed like she was fighting to sniff back tears.

"I'm used to insults from Courtney and everyone. But hearing you say you didn't think I was any good, either, and that no one would ever like me . . . it . . . I don't know. It made me . . . upset." She turned away.

I grabbed her arm. "I never said that. I never would."

"You did," she protested. "You said Cole would never be interested in someone like me."

"Gabi, I didn't mean it like that. Honest. All I meant was if he was interested in someone like klutzy, sloppy old me, then he probably wouldn't go for someone perfect like you. We're completely different. Honestly, I don't even know why he'd be interested in me with you around."

"Oh, please." She smacked my arm. But it was in a playful way, not an I-want-to-cause-you-bodily-harm way. "You're full of it. But thank you."

"I'm sorry if I hurt your feelings," I said. And I really meant it.

"And I'm sorry about the whole Cole mess. Will you forgive me?"

"It's not like I have much choice." I looked out at the crowd. "You're the only person who seems to realize I exist. And you're better than nothing!"

That last part made Gabi laugh.

"I'm going to fix everything," Gabi said. "People don't think *you* exist. So what if I give you a new identity? It'd be like starting fresh!"

My stare gave her the answer to that one.

"Well, what if I made the new you the most popular girl in school?"

"Wishing for popularity is what got us in this mess to begin with!" I said, throwing my hands in the air.

"I know. I guess I was just wanted to keep you *and* my wishes."

"Unfortunately, you really can't. It's all got to go back, the automatic As, the TV, the dessert bar in your room . . ."

"I've had more than enough ice cream, thank you very much." She glanced back at the giant bowl still sitting onstage.

"Sorry," I said. "I shouldn't have tried to embarrass you."

"And I shouldn't have danced with Cole."

I looked down at my hands. The Cole thing still hurt. "You know this reversal won't work unless you truly want to give up the wishes. Are you sure you're ready to give up being a star?"

Gabi pointed to the cameraman filming her. "In their world you don't exist. So I'm going to be the star

215

talking to an imaginary friend. Not exactly the kind of fame I was going for."

I shrugged my shoulder. "You could always wish for imaginary friends to become a trend."

She shook her head. "No. That still wouldn't give you your life back. Let's do it. Let's reverse this mess."

How could I ever have doubted her?

chapter

When Gabi really puts her mind to something, she does it. In a mere second the wishes were gone. She just had to concentrate on how much she really wanted them to disappear and snap—everything reversed itself.

Right away there was a lot of confusion. A lot of "What's going on?" and "Did you notice all the freaky stuff happening today?" and "Would they really put Gabi on TV?" buzzing throughout the audience.

One person was louder than all the rest. "Why is the nerd herd onstage?" Courtney shouted. "I thought Lance Gold was going to be here. I didn't come here to look at those two freaks."

Courtney Lourde was back! Her snotty comments never sounded so good.

Elena made her way to the stage. "There's been

a mistake. I just checked with my office. Lance was never scheduled to be here today. But he does have an appearance at the mall in Killingsworth next week, which we hope you'll attend. Now, I do have some bad news to share." She glanced down at her BlackBerry. "The network has informed me that they've decided to kill the reality show, so unfortunately none of you are going to be stars today." She nodded her head toward the door, and she and the camera crew made their exit. With Gabi's wish reversed, they had no reason to stay.

The auditorium erupted with chatter again. "This is so weird," Tracy Fine said. "First we're in a reality show starring *Gabi* and now it's canceled? All in the same day?"

Dana Ellers shrugged. "I guess Hollywood is like that. Chews you up, spits you out, that type of thing. Stinks for Gabi."

"Like she ever stood a chance at stardom," Courtney said. "I can't believe they even considered her. How much do you want to bet it was one of those extreme makeover shows, but it got canceled when Elena realized there was no helping that lost cause?"

Jaydin and Lana burst out laughing.

"Can it, Courtney," I yelled back. "You don't

know anything. Gabi will be a star someday. She's incredible."

"So incredible that Cole picked *her* over *you*," Jaydin threw in.

I had hoped no one remembered that.

"He didn't mean it," Gabi said. "But he did choose Angel over *you* at the dance."

That got Jaydin to shut up.

Cole was sitting right in the front row. His face looked like a strawberry lollipop. We made eye contact for a second, but I looked away. I wasn't ready to talk to him. Not there, not in front of everyone.

I jumped off the stage and moved toward the back. I didn't even want to see him.

Everyone was talking about what had happened today. Saying stuff like they couldn't believe they actually followed Max around. And trying to figure out how science class became an outdoor garden.

Then a rumor began circulating that the reality show was responsible for everything. That Elena had transformed the science room, painted the walls and lockers, all at super speed to help the show along. And now that it was canceled, they were undoing everything right away, so they could go back to Hollywood.

According to the gossip, the show's crew was even the reason why everyone was nice to Max. Apparently, one of the cameramen was friends with Max's dad. So he told a few people to treat Max like Mr. Popular—and if they did he'd make them look good on TV. And once a couple of kids started treating Max like royalty, it kind of caught on.

People actually seemed to buy it all. I guess people want answers. Even when they don't make sense, which was just fine by me. I actually hoped that was the case. Because, I admit it, I was the one who started the rumors.

When everyone was talking I wrote up a fake note from Elena that took responsibility for everything. Then I made sure to drop it in Tracy Fine's lap as I made my way past her. She was a huge gossip. If you ever want the whole school to know something, right away, tell Tracy Fine. It's quicker than Facebook.

Mr. Stanton entered the room, bullhorn in hand. "All right, everyone," he yelled into it, practically destroying one of my eardrums. I was right next to him. "This day has gotten out of hand. But the craziness is over."

Finally.

"Everyone is to go back to class," he ordered.

I was the first one out. But an arm grabbed me. "Just

a minute." It was Miss Spring, the evil school nurse.

"Is that my jacket?" she asked.

Oh no. No. NO. Of all the people in the whole school, why did I have to take Miss Spring's coat? The woman lived to torture students. "No," I answered.

"I don't believe you." We were drawing a crowd. "That is definitely my jacket," the nurse said, examining the fabric.

She actually reached into the coat's pocket and pulled out her sunglasses case. She pointed to the letters **DS** on the front. "Are you going to say these are your initials as well?"

Well, it could have stood for Daughter of Satan. But I decided to keep that thought to myself. "Can we talk about this in your office?" I asked.

"No," she said.

Note to self: Add Miss Spring to list of possible demons.

"It's just a big mix-up," I said.

"Hand the coat over," she said.

"I'm a little chilly. How about I give it back later?"

"Now."

I gritted my teeth and untied the jacket.

My new boobs were about to make their Goode Middle School debut.

chapter

Miss Spring took the jacket from me, and even she seemed shocked by my new appearance. For a second I thought she was actually going to hand the coat back and put me out of my misery.

"No way!" Courtney said, through fits of giggles. "So that's why there's no toilet paper left in the girls' bathroom."

"Did she really think no one would notice that she stuffed her bra?" Jaydin asked.

"It's like she shoved beach balls up her shirt," Lana chimed in.

Well, Courtney and Co. certainly were no longer nice. Not even close.

What was worse—the whole auditorium was laughing at me. At least it felt that way. I scanned the room. Oh. My. God. Everyone was looking my way.

Even Cole. I crossed my arms over my chest, turned around, and bolted straight for the exit. And not just from the auditorium—from the whole school.

And I didn't stop there. I just kept running.

"Wait up!" It was Gabi.

I stopped.

She was out of breath, and we were only a few blocks from school. She really was a horrible athlete. "Where did you get those things?" she asked, pointing right at my boobs.

I shielded them with my arms. "Target," I said.

Gabi rolled her eyes at me. "Seriously, what happened?"

"What always happens. I tried to use my powers and they went all wonky. These things"—I looked down at the massive growths coming out of my upper body—"weren't supposed to get this big. I just wanted Cole to notice me."

"I'm sure he noticed all right. I think everyone did." I couldn't tell if she said it with disbelief or awe.

"Thanks a lot."

"Sorry," she said. "It's just . . . I never saw any that big."

Gabi wasn't making me feel any better. I went

from having the flattest chest in all the land to having prize-winning watermelons.

"Why didn't you just make them small again?" she asked.

I still didn't like the term *small* used when referring to my boobs, but it beat what they were now—crazy gigantic. "Don't you think I tried?"

"If I were you, I'd try again. I don't know how you're going to explain those to your mom."

That was true. Especially since Mom didn't know about my powers. And the stuffing excuse wouldn't get me very far. As soon as she saw me trying to go to school this way, she'd demand I take the stuffing out of my bra.

"You're right. I can do this." The last time I attempted to make them shrink, I was interrupted and had to give up. This time I'd just keep trying, even if it took all night.

Go back to normal, go back to normal. Actually a little bigger than normal would be better. Go back to a little bigger than normal, I thought and pushed my arms against my chest, willing them to shrink.

But it wasn't working. Maybe because I was being greedy. But come on! I wasn't asking for the world. Just a happy medium. Not boobs that were too big. Or ones that were too small. Just something in between.

I closed my eyes again and focused really hard. I could feel my shirt getting looser. It was working!

"Uh, Angel," Gabi said. "You might want to open your eyes."

I didn't like the tone of her voice. I looked down at my chest. No way! There was something worse than having a massively small chest *or* a massively big one. And that was having *one* itty-bitty boob *and one* gargantuan one. I was completely lopsided. Only one of my boobs went back to its normal size. "This was not what I meant by having something in between!"

This was going to be really hard to explain. I had to get them back to their regular size. I covered my chest with my arms. *Fine*, I thought. *I give in. Just go back to normal. To A-cup Angel.*

I concentrated and concentrated and concentrated. Finally, I felt some movement. My big boob was getting smaller and smaller, until it was back to its original size.

"You did it!" Gabi yelled, and clapped her hands together.

Thank goodness. For once I was actually happy to see my nonexistent chest!

chapter
✦ 45 ✦

"Mom?" She wasn't in the kitchen when I got home. "Mom!" I called out again.

There still wasn't any answer. I checked the living room.

"MOM!"

"What is it?" she asked, coming down the stairs.

"Nothing." I just threw my arms around her, not caring if I seemed like the crazy one in the family this time. Having your very own flesh and blood, your own mother, even a kooky one like mine, act like you didn't exist was scary. I was just happy to have her back.

"Are you okay?"

I nodded. "Just wanted to say hello."

Mom gave me a questioning look. It wasn't every day, okay, any day, that I came home and ran straight to hug her. She squeezed me back. "Sure you're okay?" she asked as I pulled away.

She wasn't getting any more info out of me. After one last hug, I ran to my room and closed the door. "You've got mail! You've got mail! You've got mail! You've got mail!" a voice said, which was very strange. Even if my e-mail account could still have been open from this morning, I didn't have AOL.

It had to be Lou.

I picked up my computer. Not because I wanted to know what he had to say. He was out of my life. I just wanted the noise to stop.

When I logged on to my e-mail account, just like I suspected, the message at the top of my inbox was from Lou. It was a memo to everyone in the underworld, and he had bcc'd me on it. Basically it warned that if anyone attempted to take a good soul, they'd get in huge trouble.

After I read it, the memo dissolved off the screen. In its place was a live video feed from Lou. "Did you read my note?" he asked.

"Yeah, but it doesn't change anything. I'm not forgiving you."

"There's more," he said, sounding like one of those infomercial guys who keep throwing in more incentives to get you to buy their knives or potato peelers.

Lou held up a piece of paper and ripped it in half. As he did it went up in flames. "That was the contract Gremory made for the soul of the baseball player." He ripped a few more pieces of paper, sending more flames into the air. "And these are a few old contracts I made years ago. I convinced them to trade in their wishes in exchange for their souls. I'm cleaning up my act. Because of you."

I didn't know what to say.

"Do you forgive me?"

"No," I said. It was great that he sent out the memo and all, but I still didn't trust him. How did I know that he wouldn't just go and send out a revised note the next day, taking back what he'd just said? Or that he'd ripped up real contracts and not some scrap paper with special effects thrown in? "How would I have known if any of it was true?"

"You can check," he said. "I'll e-mail you a list of names. Just Google them. You'll see. Then after you know it's the real deal, we'll be okay, right?"

"I'm sorry," I said. "I can't do it anymore."

"Angel."

"No, Lou. You messed up big time."

"You mean like accidentally making all of your best friend's wishes come true?" he asked.

"I don't know what you're talking about," I lied.

A moment later a video came up on my screen of Lou vanishing into thin air from my school hallway, a zombie coming for me, and me running like crazy.

"Yeah, you don't remember that?" Lou asked, his face reappearing on the screen. He looked amused.

"How'd you get that?"

"I have my ways."

"Did you hurt the camera guy?" I yelled at him.

"Of course not," he said. "But there was no way I'd risk that footage getting out."

I bit my nail. "How did you even know there was footage?"

"Angel," he said, shaking his head. "You don't think I knew something was up? You're not as good a liar as you think."

Maybe that was a good thing. I didn't want to be like him.

"When I ran into you and Gabi, I could tell you granted her wishes. Your body language, your voice, the look in your friend's eyes. I've been doing this a long time. I have a sixth sense for this type of thing."

"Why didn't you say anything?" I asked.

"You didn't want my help. And sometimes the best way to learn is by fixing your own mistakes." He gave me a small smile. "And that's what I'm trying to do, too. Fix my mistakes. Please, Angel, forgive me. Give me another chance."

I wanted to believe him. I wanted to forgive him. But I had already given him so many chances. I wasn't falling for it again. I was done playing the fool. "I'm sorry," I said. "I can't." I closed the laptop.

My time with the devil was over.

chapter 46

"It looks like Lou did give back those souls," I told Gabi as we walked into the cafeteria the next day. "It was all over the Web. That baseball player got kicked off the team. A billionaire business guy went bankrupt. A NASCAR racer got his driver's license taken away. The list goes on and on."

"So are you going to forgive him?" she asked as we sat down at our table.

"Yeah . . . eventually. I just need to see that he's really given up trading souls. Once I'm convinced I'm sure I'll feel differently."

"But you do forgive me, right? We're okay?"

I nodded. "We're more than okay."

"Good," she said, looking into her lunch bag. "In that case, any chance you want to give me back those wishes? Today I have tofu pastrami on seven-grain bread with a side of dried apples. Yuck. That cheeseburger was a lot better."

"Not a chance," I said. But I did hand her one of my Oreos.

Gabi twisted it open. "I figured as much. I guess I sort of went overboard at the end there."

"You think?"

"I'm sorry I got all crazy," she said.

"Don't forget mean," I told her.

"And mean." She bit her lip. "You're never going to let me forget this, are you?"

"Probably not." I threw my napkin at her. "But we're even now. You forgave me after I was stupid enough to pick Courtney over you, now it's my turn to hand out the forgiveness."

I was just glad to have Gabi back. We were even able to joke about things that didn't seem so funny yesterday (i.e., that small island that was growing out of my chest). I knew people were going to be trash talkin' me about it for years to come.

"Hey," Cole said, taking a cautious step toward me. I had been avoiding him again. It was all so humiliating.

He looked at me, then Gabi, then back at me. "Did you get my messages?"

Cole had called and left about a dozen voicemails

apologizing over and over again. He even left a corny note taped to my locker—which didn't seem so corny because it was addressed to me—begging me to forgive him.

"Yeah," I said.

"I don't know what came over me. I don't know why I sent those notes to Gabi or that cupcake or any of it." Cole's head dropped down.

I kind of wanted to make him sweat it out. After all, he did pick my best friend over me. Even if it wasn't really his fault.

"I'm so sorry," he said, lifting only his eyes, "to both of you."

He kicked a napkin on the floor. "Angel, do you think—" He paused. "Do you think you can forgive me?" It seemed everyone was asking me that.

Cole looked genuinely sad. And to be fair he only chose Gabi because of my powers. That didn't make it hurt any less. But I said yes because the thought of losing him hurt a lot more.

He looked up and smiled at me. One of those cute, lopsided grins I thought I'd never see again. At least not directed at me. "I'll make it up to you. I promise," he said. "You still want to go see *Zombie Zone Four* with me tomorrow?"

I'd had my fill of zombies. Enough to last me the rest of my life. But I could definitely deal with another hour and a half of them as long as Cole was sitting by my side.

"Yeah," I said, smiling back at him. "But, I have to warn you, zombies make me scream."

"I'll be there to protect you," he said.

My stomach did a few jumping jacks.

Gabi made a gagging noise. "Just kidding," she said. "It's sweet."

Cole blushed. "I told Reid I'd sit with him today," he said, looking back at his friend. Cole was definitely looking for an escape. The whole situation was still a little weird. He didn't seem quite sure what to say to Gabi. Not after what happened. And not with me sitting right there. "Is that okay?"

"Of course," I said.

He put his hand on mine and left it there for a second. "Wait for me after lunch. We'll walk to next period together."

I nodded.

Then he walked away. But he smiled at Gabi first. I wasn't going to let it make me jealous. It was just a smile. A smile at someone he had said he always thought was pretty. But that didn't really bother me. Gabi *was* pretty.

"Hey," I said once Cole was gone, "have you talked to Marc?"

"He won't even look at me now that the wish wore off." Gabi picked at her sandwich and tried to smile. But it looked forced. My next project was totally going to be finding her a boyfriend. She deserved to find someone awesome like Cole—just not Cole himself!

"He's nuts. You're going to find someone better, I promise."

"Too bad Elena left before she introduced me to Lance Gold. Now that would have been cool!"

"Totally."

But I would take Cole over Lance any day. I couldn't keep myself from sneaking a few extra glimpses at him during the rest of lunch. He was back at his old table. D.L. caught me looking over, but instead of making fun of me—he actually smiled. But it's possible he was just thinking about how ridiculous I looked the other day. I quickly turned back to Gabi.

We had another visitor a moment later. Courtney. I should have known I wouldn't make it through lunch without having a run-in with her. Life was definitely back to normal.

"Hi," she said. "I think . . ." Then she lifted one hand to her nose and pretended to sneeze. "Double-A

235

choo," she said, while flinging a handful of tissues at me with her other hand. She picked one of them up by two fingers and held it in the air so everyone could see. "You're leaking, Angel. The bathroom's restocked, if you need to freshen up your bra."

"Ha-ha," I said. I was going to be the school laughingstock forever.

Courtney turned to go back to her table. But we both were surprised by what we saw. Max—the nerdy version—had taken her seat.

"What is *he* doing?!" Courtney yelled, and stomped back to her table.

"Committing social suicide," Gabi answered more to herself than anyone else.

My whole body tensed up. "Did we mess up? Does he think he's still welcome there?"

"I don't know," Gabi said.

We both watched, waiting for the worst.

"Why are you here?" Courtney hovered over him.

"I told you," Jaydin answered for him. "I'm his new tutor."

Courtney put her hands on her hips. "Why?"

Jaydin shrugged. "I don't know. I said I would. And it'll look good on my transcript. You know my mom is bugging me about doing more extracurricular activities." For a second she reminded me of Gabi.

"Well, he's in my seat," Courtney fumed. She gave Max a disgusted glance. "He's not welcome at this table."

"Fine," Jaydin said, getting up. "We'll work over there."

Courtney's jaw dropped. "You're picking that *thing* over sitting with me?!"

"It's for school," Jaydin practically screamed. "Besides, it's only a couple of days a week. He's going to work with his other tutor the rest of the time. So lay off. Let's go, Max."

Jaydin moved to an empty table and Max followed her. And it might have been my imagination, but I was pretty sure he was standing a little straighter.

"Whoa," Gabi said.

"Tell me about it. Maybe we did some good after all."

And as I watched Max take his seat and actually smile, I was sure of it. Which made the whole big mess 150 percent worth it.

Shani Petroff is a writer living in New York City. *Bedeviled: Careful What You Wish For* is the third book in the Bedeviled series. She also writes for news programs and several other venues. When she's not locked in her apartment typing away, she spends a whole lot of time on books, boys, TV, daydreaming, and shopping online. She'd love for you to come visit her at www.shanipetroff.com.

bedeviled

LOVE STRUCK

Will Angel's powers ever stop
getting her into trouble?

 Find out in the next
installment of Bedeviled:
Love Struck